I0601179

WOLF PACK
THE BROTHER'S CREED BOOK 3
JOSHUA C. CHADD

BLADE OF TRUTH PUBLISHING COMPANY

Published in the United States by Blade of Truth Publishing Company

Cover art by Stefan Celic

Contact the author via email at: author@joshuacchadd.com

ISBN: 978-1-64248-003-0

Apocalypse Road Trip Playlist

This playlist was spawned as I listened to music while writing *Outbreak*. Before long, some of the songs found their way into the book itself. As the story continued, music took on a bigger role, even inspiring not one but two titles and some key themes woven throughout the series. The playlist has since grown as I continue to add more and is my go-to when writing apocalyptic stories. Music is powerful and has a way to inspire and motivate when other things fall short. As Connor says in *Last Hope*:

> "Some thought it odd how much they loved music, but what they didn't understand was that these songs were more than just melodies; they were expressions of emotions when they couldn't express any themselves. Music had helped them through some hard times, even before the apocalypse. It wasn't just about the tunes or even the lyrics, but rather what they represented. It was a celebration of what made them human."

Scan the QR code or visit the URL to be taken to the official ***Apocalypse Road Trip Playlist*** and listen along with the group as they embark on a road trip through the apocalypse!

https://spoti.fi/2SB9jKM

Oh man, what can I say?

There have been times when I've wanted to kill you, and when you have almost killed me. We've gone months without talking when life was busy, we've fought, gotten pissed at each other, drifted apart and then back together, liked the same girls, hated the same asshats, and endured the same horror story that was high school.

Through it all, we've not only stayed best friends but grown our friendship to the brotherhood it is today. You are my oldest friend and we're going on a decade and a half. And this is just the beginning!

Caleb and I will always have your back and I know you have ours. We will always be the original Wolf Pack!
This one's for you, Andy!

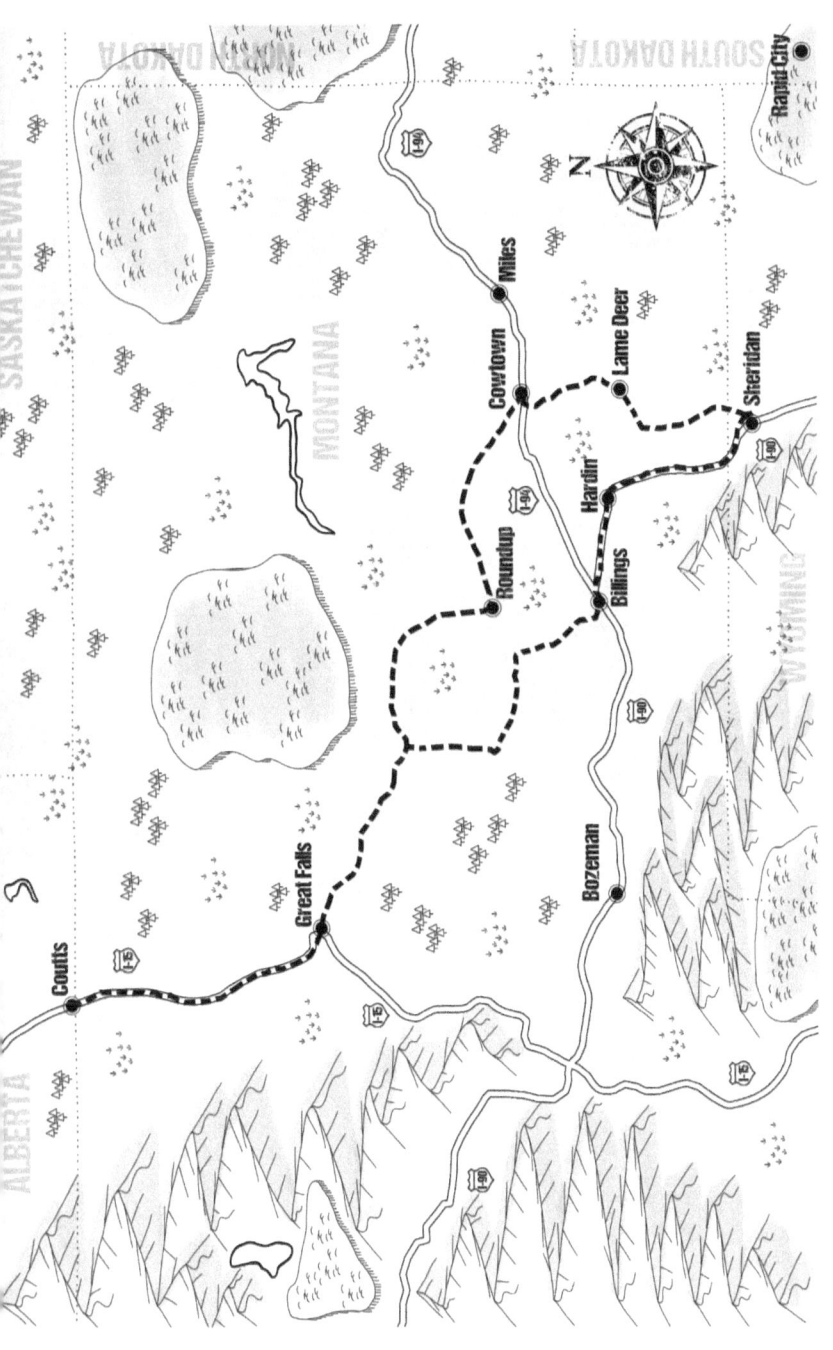

1

BOXES

E xhausted, Ana leaned against the wooden pole as the cold ground sapped the warmth from her legs. She'd tried everything she could think of to free herself, but it'd proven useless. Even with all of Uncle Zeke's training, she hadn't been able to so much as loosen the shackles. These people knew how to properly keep captives. Her mind flashed back to situations in her life that were similar to this, but with her on the other side.

Remove that thought, said Uncle Zeke's voice in her mind, an echo from one of their training sessions.

She'd always been good at controlling her thoughts, even before she'd started training with him. Her mind began to drift back to the first memory she'd locked away as a child. It was a cold January day in New York City. Her father, Vadim, had gone up to meet the *Pakhan* of a rival family, bringing her mother, Natta, and her with him. Little did she know the event would change the course of her life forever...

Ana looked around, disoriented. Was this some kind of barn she was in? Why was she chained up? Her current situation began to break through like fog burning away in the hot sun; she realized she'd had another incident. It tended to happen when she let herself think back to—

Remove that thought! said Uncle Zeke's voice again in her mind.

She immediately closed her eyes and instinctively reached to rub the small golden locket around her neck, tucked under her gray, long-sleeved shirt, but the chains kept her hands from reaching it. Taking deep breaths, she emptied her mind, putting all her thoughts and emotions into neat boxes. She could visualize them—black, unmarked boxes of varying sizes.

Sometime later, she opened her eyes. All of her memories were back where they belonged. Feeling the shackles locked around her wrists, she searched for a chip or crack, any weakness she could exploit. The length of the chains made it impossible for her and the others to stand. It kept them all seated with their hands behind their backs—a technique that made it almost impossible to resist their captors. As she worked on the chains, another part of her mind worked on a way to get out of there. First, she'd have to free herself. Then she could wait by the door, take down a guard, steal a weapon, and fight her way out, killing everyone who got in her way.

She glanced at the other men and women being held captive in the barn. Would she take the time to help them or just get out? If she went alone, there was a good chance she would get away, but if she freed them all, there was no way they'd make it without a fight. After brief consideration, she decided she wouldn't worry about these people. They'd gotten themselves into this position in the first place, they could get themselves out.

But what about Alexis? asked a voice in her mind.

Emmett and Alexis had rescued her from the mall and she owed them a debt that couldn't go unpaid. That wasn't the way things worked. She would help Alexis; the rest would be on their own.

Loyalty to your family, Zeke's voice said.

Alexis and Emmett were family now. The brothers had helped her, too, so they were included, but not the rest. The rest were just a liability. Why had James insisted on helping the survivors from Burns? It made their entire group weaker.

Even though the five of them had only been together for a day, she could tell they made a great team. But this thought took her back to her two bodyguards who'd given their lives for her in the mall—Viktor and Hagen. They'd been like the brothers she'd never had. Her fingers tried to find their way to her locket again as her mind worked to put those memories back into their respective boxes. She released a pent-up breath, feeling exhausted. She hadn't thought this much about the past since the beginning of the outbreak. With her mind focused on surviving for one more day, it had been easy to keep the past from coming back to haunt her. There was no telling what her mind would drift back to with all this time alone.

She attacked the chains with ferocity, needing to be free of these bonds or risk going insane. She *had* to get out of there, and quickly, before that psychopath came back. Just thinking about Jezz brought a shiver to her spine. Ana had seen her for what she was the moment Jezz had walked into the barn the night before—a killer. And not someone who killed for work or to survive. Not even like Father Ahaz, who never dirtied his own hands but let his pet zombies take care of it. No, this woman was a true killer, someone who believed she was truly helping them, in some sick way, by killing them. Ana had known someone like this before, but she closed that box before the memory could resurface. She knew she was in extreme danger as long as she was trapped here.

A sound drew her attention to the door as it opened and daylight streamed into the barn. Was it morning already? The sun was still rising, so it was early. Two guards stood on the other side of the door, facing away. They weren't worried about the prisoners at all.

The monster known as Jezz walked into the room, midnight black hair framing a pretty face, and closed the door behind her.

"Good morning, my dears," Jezz said, smiling sweetly.

No one answered as she slithered by Alexis to stand a few feet in front of Ana in the middle of the barn. She began to spin in a slow circle, looking intently at all the captives. Her eyes shone with an intensity that discomfited Ana. It was like she was searching for the ripest apple to pluck from the tree and devour.

Ana shivered.

"Ah, now *this one* will do," Jezz said.

She began to walk toward Ana, an animalistic hunger in her eyes. Ana's mind worked in overtime. She had to get out of there or this woman was going to kill her. Struggling with her shackles, her skin started bleeding again where she'd rubbed her wrists raw. Jezz drew closer and Ana's attempts to escape grew more frantic as tears threatened to leak from her eyes. This couldn't be the end. She hated her show of weakness and tried to force the tears and terror back down.

Jezz walked past her, kneeling down next to a woman at the edge of the large barn. Ana let out a ragged breath, Jezz wasn't coming for her after all. She knew it was only a matter of time until they were all dead, but this gave her more time to plan an escape—more time to live.

"What is your name, my dear?" Jezz asked, caressing the cheek of the brunette-haired woman. Ana closed her eyes, not wanting to see what Jezz was going to do next.

"Mmm... Mmm..." The woman's voice was quivering so much that she couldn't speak.

"Spit it out," Jezz said harshly, her demeanor changing in an instant.

"Margaret," the brunette woman finally said, her voice full of fear.

"Ah, what a nice name. Would you like to be our first guest, Margaret?"

"Guest? For what?"

"It's a surprise, but I promise you will like it."

"I... I..." Margaret began to cry—deep body-wracking sobs.

Ana could hear the fear and desperation in those sobs. She felt a little sorry for the woman but quickly stuffed that down. These people were just liabilities, nothing else. If she grew attached to them, it'd ruin her plan to escape. There was no way to save them all.

"Oh, dear. What is this? Did you soil yourself?" Jezz asked a hysterical Margaret. "That will not do; that will not do at all."

Though she'd closed her eyes against the scene that had begun to play out, Ana heard Jezz get up and begin to walk back toward the middle of the barn. Ana didn't open her eyes. She didn't want to see that monster. Boots crunched softly on the gravel behind Ana as Jezz drew near.

She's not coming for me, Ana thought desperately, *she can't be.*

The room was suddenly silent.

"You, my dear, are perfect," Jezz said from right in front of her.

Ana's eyes shot open, her gaze immediately finding the black-haired woman looking down at her with hungry blue eyes.

2

TOGETHER TILL THE END

Post-outbreak day 6, late evening

James stood in the back of the bus with the note clenched in a white-knuckled grip, Hank's naked body staked to the back door in front of him. Rain continued to pound the roof and the noise reverberated throughout the bus. Connor stood a few feet behind James, facing the door. Even now, his brother was ready for anything and here he was with tears streaming down his cheeks. He'd failed them. He'd failed them all. He was the one who'd convinced them to leave the school in Burns and head north. He was the one who'd gotten them here. It was like some twisted nightmare he couldn't wake up from. The guilt ate at him as he stood there, engrossed in his dark thoughts. They never should've tried to help these people. They would've been better off back at the school.

"Is not your fault, bro," Connor said. "I know that's what you're thinkin', but it's not."

"How the hell do you figure that?" James asked, turning to face his brother.

"Because you're not responsible for these people," Connor said. "They *chose* to follow you; you didn't force them. You just told them what needed to be done and they listened. Just because they followed you doesn't make you responsible. You have to get that through your thick skull."

"Why are we even having this conversation again?"

"Because you just don't seem to get it. People make their own choices in life and they have to live with those choices. They'd all be dead if it wasn't for us—for you. They're still out there, James—Olive, Emmett, Alexis, Ana, and the rest. You've got to hold it together long enough for us to find them. Don't think about the ones we've lost; think about the ones we still have."

He's right, of course, James thought.

He couldn't just stand there having a pity party. They had to rescue their friends or give themselves up in order to save the rest. Olive's smiling face flashed through his mind and his protective instinct flared to life. Was she okay? If she was dead, he would never forgive himself. He would go to the ends of the earth to find her and make sure she was safe. He had to hold it together, at least until then.

"Okay," James said, sighing.

"I need you, James," Connor said, walking over to him. "You, me, and Tank—we're the only family we have left. We have to stick together or none of us will make it."

Connor embraced him. Reluctantly, James hugged him back. The tears began again, but he wasn't ashamed of them. After a brief moment, they separated, looking each other in the eyes.

"I got your six," James said. "I'm not giving up, not by a long shot."

"Good, because we have some work ahead of us."

Connor exited the bus, returning to the Hummer parked outside, and James glanced back at Hank's body. He knew his brother was right—he couldn't take the blame for this, but that didn't stop the guilty thoughts from gnawing at him. He was at least partially responsible for this, but he would deal with that later. For now, he had to pull himself together. They had friends to rescue and people to kill.

James followed Connor out of the bus and climbed into the back seat of the Hummer. It wasn't until he was in the warm interior that he realized how cold he was. All of his clothing was soaked, and he was chilled to the bone. His ear and side ached, and the water stung the small cuts on his face.

"So what's the plan now?" Tank asked.

"We have to discuss it," James said with a shiver. "We found a note from the Reclaimers in the bus. They have the rest of our group."

"What does it say?" Chloe asked.

James unfolded the crumpled paper that was speckled with blood. "I have your friends," he read. "I will kill one every twelve hours until you arrive. Come unarmed and in plain sight. If I even *think* you are planning a rescue, I will kill them all, starting with the little ones. You have to pay for what you have done, the lives you have taken. I am waiting, J."

Everyone sat in silence for a few moments. The wind howled and rain still covered the landscape, but the lightning had moved on. They were past the heart of the storm.

"Well, hell," Tank said. "Looks like this just got a whole lot worse."

"Yeah," James said, "but they're our people, so I understand if you don't wanna help us."

"What the hell do ya mean?" Tank asked. "Wherever you guys go, I go. The Wolf Pack isn't splitting up again. We're in this thing together, till the end."

"I couldn't have said it any better myself," James said. "Chloe?"

"It's not like I'm gonna let you guys leave me out here somewhere," Chloe said. "I'm just not any good with guns and I don't know if I can kill anyone."

"That's okay," James said. "We'll leave you with the rig. You can be our getaway driver."

"I can do that," Chloe said.

"So what's the play?" Tank asked.

"I really have no idea," James said, "but I know we'll figure it out. For now, we need to find somewhere safe where we can come up with a plan."

"Good idea," Tank said, "because I feel like a sittin' chicken out here."

"A sittin' chicken?" Connor asked.

"Yeah, a sittin' chicken," Tank said. "I figured a chicken was a little more vulnerable than a duck. A duck can fly off whenever it wants, but a chicken, well, that thing's just screwed when it's out in the open."

James couldn't help but laugh. The situation was far from humorous, but he laughed anyway, and it felt good. Their friends were in grave danger—in fact, they were all in danger. Still, he needed to remember to live in each moment; otherwise, what kind of existence would that be? As the laughter quieted, James realized his brother was right—again. Everyone made their own choices. It was Tank's choice to follow them, not his and not his brother's. He couldn't take that choice away from Tank and claim responsibility for his actions. That was up to him alone. Just like Peter and the group had decided to follow them. They'd made their choice, and even though it'd cost some their lives, it had been their choice to make. James still felt somewhat responsible. He always would, but it couldn't all be on him. That kind of responsibility would break him. He had enough troubles to deal with as it was and he didn't need to add to them.

"I guess it's time we decide where to go," Connor said.

"Yeah, I don't wanna be a sittin' chicken," Tank said, smiling.

"Let's head back toward Sheridan and take the first exit east. Find a house out there to set up in until we figure out what to do," James said.

"Sounds like a plan," Tank said, stepping on the gas and turning the Hummer around.

Cold by Five Finger Death Punch played through the speakers as the empty bus disappeared into the darkness behind them. James left some of his guilt with that bus. The rest he would carry with him until the day he died.

Since this time they weren't being shot at and chased by Reclaimers, it took them longer to get back to the turnoff for US-14. Arriving at the exit, Tank turned onto the highway, heading southeast. They passed a bunch of houses and subdivisions on the outskirts of town, taking the first dirt road on the left, which led them to a house with some outbuildings hidden among the cottonwood trees. Pulling up in front of the house, the Hummer rolled to a stop. James and Connor climbed out first, scanning their surroundings.

"Looks clear," Connor said.

"Same here," James said from the other side.

Chloe climbed out of the backseat and Tank came around to help her.

"Thanks," Chloe said, reluctantly.

"Don't mention it, babe," Tank said.

Chloe rolled her eyes. "My ankle should be fine now."

"Might as well take it easy for a bit longer," Tank said. "Let it heal fully."

"Fine, you can help me, but just watch your hands," Chloe said.

"Oh, I will," Tank said, winking.

Chloe shook her head, but she let Tank help her out of the Hummer. Stepping down, she kept the weight off her left ankle.

"You two wait out here," James said, walking over to join his brother, who was facing the house. "We'll check inside."

James switched to his 1911 handgun and led the way. Connor followed and they posted up outside the front door, James entering the building first. His handgun swept the interior, flashlight attached on the bottom, cutting through the darkness. A zombie came at him from the kitchen in front of him and he fired. A muffled crack sounded through the house as the zombie fell to the ground, the hole in its head slowly oozing blood. He stepped over the corpse as he entered the living room, his brother following him. They cleared it then Connor nodded, pointing to the hallway they'd passed on their way in.

James led the way as they moved to the hall. There were three doors—one at the end and two on the right. They went to the first one, James entering as Connor opened the door. James swept into the room, handgun leading the way. The bedroom was clear and they moved back out into the hallway. Moving to the next door on the right, James once more waited as his brother opened it, and then he burst into the room. Three small, half-eaten bodies lay on the floor. Blood covered the back wall and the two twin beds. A small zombie came at him, but he didn't notice it.

James was no longer there, he was back in the house in Meriden. Fourteen little bodies were scattered around the room in various states of being consumed. Blood covered everything. One little girl with black hair was still alive, hiding under the bed. On the other side, a zombie clawed at her, trying to reach her. She cried, scooting farther from the zombie. It fell to its belly and started to crawl under the bed after the girl. She whimpered and scrambled out from under the bed, running for the door. She tried to open it, but it was locked. James had told them to lock it. She fumbled with the knob. Finally, she got it unlocked and started to twist the knob, but it was too late. The zombie rose from under the bed and descended on the girl. She tried to scream but the zombie ripped into her neck. Blood splattered the door as she was taken to the floor.

Something pulled James from behind and he fell. He blinked, trying to figure out where he was. He was in a hallway looking into a room where his brother had just taken down a small zombie with his tomahawk. Connor turned around and stared at James, his expression shifting from concern to anger. He came over to James and offered his hand. James took it and his brother hauled him to his feet. He'd just had another episode and almost been bitten. The small zombie lay on the ground not a foot from the doorway. It would've had to have been only inches from him when Connor pulled him back.

"Get a grip, James," Connor said, looking his brother in the eyes.

"I'm trying," James said.

"Stop trying! You either get a grip now or you get yourself and others killed." Connor said.

James hung his head. It was hard enough fighting zombies and the Reclaimers; he didn't need his own mind against him. He just didn't have the strength to fight enemies within *and* without.

"I'll take point from now on," Connor said.

His brother moved to the last room at the end of the hall, leaving James standing there. Connor opened the door and cleared the room by himself, taking down two zombies. How were they ever going to take on the Reclaimers when he kept having these episodes? It was simple: they weren't. If they tried to fight, they would all die. Every last one of them. Connor walked by, giving him a pat on the shoulder, and James followed him back to the entrance.

"The house is clear," Connor said as they walked back to the Hummer.

"Perfect," Tank said. "I'm about done with surprises today."

James walked in front of Tank, who helped Chloe inside the house. Connor brought up the rear. As they entered, James took them to the first room, not glancing down the hall to the next room. This was the master bedroom, with a king-size bed and connecting bathroom. Tank took Chloe to the bed and she sat down.

"And this is where the magic happens," Tank said, winking at Chloe.

"You're such a pig," Chloe said.

"Will you two cut it out?" Connor said, walking into the room. He closed the door behind him and sat down in a chair.

James sat on the floor, resting his AR on his lap. "So, now that we're here, what do we do?"

Tank shrugged.

"I think it'd be best if we just turned ourselves over. Do as the note says," James said.

"What the hell are you smokin'?" Connor asked. "We can't just surrender."

"Yeah, what badass movie ever has the heroes surrendering?" Tank said. "I'll tell you—none. And what kind of video game would have the heroes just give up when they're faced with tough situations?"

"I hate to break it to you," James said, "but we're not in a video game. This is real life. You know that."

"Tank does have a point," Connor said. "Since when have we ever given up?"

"They do have a lot of people," Chloe said.

"Exactly! And we're almost out of ammo," James said. "We don't have the manpower or firepower we need. If we try anything, we'll get ourselves and the others killed."

"Why are we even discussing *if* we attack or not?" Tank asked. "We should be planning *how* we're gonna attack. When I said I was with you guys, I didn't mean I was gonna go in with my tail between my legs. Ready for them to shoot us. I meant I was with you to fight. If you guys are surrendering, I'm out. I didn't survive this long just to give up."

"We're not gonna give up," Connor said. "We just need to figure this out."

James didn't *want* to give up, but he couldn't, for the life of him, figure out how they were going to plan a successful rescue. It would be one thing if they had his truck and whole arsenal, or Emmett with them; however, on their own, with hardly any ammunition? Facing a group of that many people and that much firepower would be suicidal. So what could they do? Whatever it was would need to be quick. They only had a few hours left to figure it out before whoever "J" was would start killing their people.

"Okay," James said, "we're not surrendering. The Reclaimers would probably just kill us and them anyway. It's not worth that risk."

"The note said they would kill someone every twelve hours, right?" Tank asked. "Do you know what time they were captured?"

"Shortly after they left us, more than likely," James said.

"So twelve hours would be...?" Chloe asked.

"Sunrise," Connor said, "about five-thirty."

"So what are we gonna do?" James asked.

"Kill 'em all," Tank said.

"Well, yeah," James said, "but how? We don't even know what their hideout looks like or how big their group is."

"We need to scout it out," Connor said, standing, "but first we need to find some ammo."

"And we need to hurry," James said. "We only have a few hours."

"Then what the hell are we doin' just sittin' here?" Tank said. "Let's get our asses movin'!"

3

A CHOICE

Ana looked into those blue eyes and felt fear like she hadn't in years. This woman was going to kill her and there was nothing she could do about it. With that thought, she steeled herself. If this was really the end, she wasn't going to go out begging or crying. She would go out with her back straight, staring into the eyes of her murderer.

"If you're going to kill me," Ana said, "then just do it. I'm tired of your games."

"Games? What games?" Jezz asked.

"Whatever this sick game is you're playing," Ana said. "Quit trying to scare us. I'm not afraid of you."

Ana stared her in the eyes, trying to hide the fear in her own. This woman was exactly like her mother...

Her mind went blank.

Ana blinked. It'd happened again. Something about today causing her to remember things she'd locked away years ago, memories she hadn't thought about in a lifetime. She had to do something. She couldn't let herself be killed by someone like this.

"Oh, but you *are* afraid," Jezz said, smiling, "and you should be."

"Just do it," Ana said, staring daggers.

"Your time will come," Jezz said, turning and striding through the barn. She knocked on the door and a man opened it from the outside. She turned back into the barn and pointed at Ana.

"That is the one," Jezz said. "Bring her."

Jezz strode through the doorway, disappearing outside, and the man headed straight for Ana. He was a burly man with cold eyes and a flat face—Max. The one who'd led the ambush and captured them.

"No!" Alexis shouted as Max walked by her.

He didn't even glance in her direction but kept moving forward with purpose, his eyes locked on Ana. There was no way she was getting out of this one. After all she'd been through, after all she'd survived, to end up like this. She almost wished her mother had just...

No, I won't think like that.

Max went around the back of the post and unlocked her chains, taking hold of them. He prodded her in the back and she started walking toward the exit.

"Please, no," Alexis said in a hushed voice.

As Ana walked by Alexis, their eyes locked and a look passed between them.

"Goodbye," Ana whispered.

Alexis opened her mouth to say something, but Max pushed Ana forward. He brought her outside and she blinked at the sudden brightness.

As soon as her eyes adjusted, she looked around, drinking in her surroundings. The sun was just beginning to rise over the horizon to her right. This would be her last sunrise. She took a moment and memorized the complimentary reds, oranges, and pinks painting the sky. She'd never seen a sunrise so beautiful and didn't know if it was because it was her last or because the sunrises in this country were that much better than on the east coast.

Pulling her eyes away from the horizon, she continued to look around. To her right sat a small pond, the light breeze creating ripples on the surface. A hundred yards in front of her were a couple of buildings. They had cream-colored siding and dark green roofs: a house and a detached garage. On her left, a red dirt driveway snaked down the small hill leading to more buildings. Looking behind her, she confirmed that is was a large pole barn they'd been held in. Two guards stood outside the door, one looking at her with obvious eagerness and the other not looking at her at all. Judging by all the buildings and fences, she guessed this was a ranch they were on. It sat in a small valley surrounded by mostly barren hills, like the country around Sheridan they'd been driving through before the ambush.

It'd only been a short ride from the interstate last night when they'd been brought here, so they probably weren't far from town. They should have been more prepared. If they'd been ready for it, maybe they could've... No need to think about that now. What's done was done.

Jezz stood in front of the pole barn, a predatory smile on her face, and Max brought Ana to stand before her. A dozen armed men and women stood around them, aiming at her. Max let go of her chains and went back toward the barn.

Ana locked gazes with Jezz. She would not go out whimpering.

"You *are* a fiery one," Jezz said.

Ana continued to stare. Thoughts clawed at her mind, trying to get out of the boxes they were locked in, but she didn't let them out. Now, of all times, she would *not* let them out. Her mind worked through plan after plan, but she knew it was hopeless. There was no way out of this. There were too many guards, they were too well armed, and the woman in front of her was a time bomb waiting to blow.

Jezz just stood there and continued to smile.

"Are you going to do it or not?" Ana said, frustrated by the mounting anxiety inside her.

"In time," Jezz responded.

Ana heard whimpering behind her and glanced back. Max had returned and he had someone with him. Dragging the woman by her short blonde hair, he threw her down between Ana and Jezz. Max then went over to stand next to Jezz, drawing his handgun. The woman's glasses were askew and her hazel eyes were brimming with tears. It was Mila—the flirtatious woman who had a thing for James. Ana hadn't interacted with her much, but she knew Mila had a good heart. Why had Jezz brought her out, too?

Jezz sneered down at Mila and she lowered her gaze, beginning to cry softly. Ana didn't blame her. She wanted to cry, too, but she wouldn't give Jezz the satisfaction.

"Now, here is how this works," Jezz said. "Time is up. It has been twelve hours and one of you has to die."

Jezz walked back to one of the guards in the ring around them, and the guard handed Jezz a handgun. It was a Glock 17. Ana would know; it was one of her favorites. Returning to the prisoners, Jezz racked a round into the chamber and then removed the magazine, looking directly at Ana.

"This is the fun part," Jezz said, her eyes twinkling. "The choice: Join us or die."

Ana's mind reeled. Join them? How could she join them? They were nothing but a group of murderers led by a psychopath. Was death really better than joining them? There was always a cost for something like this. What would be the cost of a life? Her life? At that moment, she decided to do whatever was necessary to survive. She would live, and then she would kill the monster standing before her.

"I see you begin to understand the stakes are high," Jezz said. "I will make it simple for you. Kill this woman and join us. You get to live. Or I will kill you both."

Ana glanced down at Mila, who looked up at her, tears streaking down her face. Mila didn't deserve this. She was kind-hearted and brave, and she didn't have any black marks in her past. Mila didn't deserve to die. Ana, on the other hand... *she* deserved to die. But Mila didn't get to choose. Ana did.

"You don't have to do this," Mila whispered, looking at her with pleading eyes.

Kill Mila? Kill someone else to save her own life? She didn't have any attachments to Mila whatsoever, but she *was* one of her group and Ana wondered if she could really kill her to save her own life. The real question was: if Ana *did* survive, could she live with herself after this? If she joined them, she'd be free to plan, and there was a possibility that she could save the rest. Sacrifice one to save them all? Not that she cared about them all—just Alexis. A debt had to be paid.

Jezz stood there, handgun held by the barrel, grip towards Ana. "And do not get any ideas," Jezz said, nodding at Max. "If you try anything, he will kill you and your whole group. I know I said that I would only kill one every twelve hours, but if you force me, I will reclaim them all."

"Please," Mila said, glancing at Jezz. "It doesn't have to be this way."

Jezz ignored Mila. Her eyes were locked on Ana.

A guard came over with a key and removed Ana's shackles. The chains fell to the gravel with a metallic clash. She was free and she had a choice to make—one decision that would define the rest of her life: kill to live, or die. Ana took two steps towards Jezz, the handgun within easy reach as her mind tried to reconcile it. Could she really do it? The woman kneeling before her had hopes, fears, and dreams of her own. She was a living, breathing person, a good person. While the woman holding the handgun was a monster, someone who deserved death. Was she fast enough to kill Jezz? Would it matter if she did? With one bullet she could decide her own fate and the fate of another. If she wanted to live through the day, the cost of her continued survival was one life. A life taken for a life gained.

In one quick, fluid motion, Ana grabbed the handgun, aimed, and pulled the trigger.

4

PREPARATION

Post-outbreak day 6, late night

C onnor nodded to his brother. James opened the door and Connor shouldered his rifle, easing into the room. Looking around, he quickly surmised that this was the two-car garage they'd seen from outside. He swept into the room, checking all the corners and shadows with the flashlight attached to the rail of his 1911 handgun. The last room in the house was clear.

Connor cursed, lowering his handgun. "Nothing."

"There has to be something here!" James exclaimed, moving to the empty shelving against the wall.

This was the second subdivision they'd checked, containing dozens of houses. And still, they were completely empty-handed. This wasn't going at all how they'd expected. They'd spent three hours searching and for nothing. Time was running out.

"Son of a—" James yelled, pushing the empty shelving over. "There's nothing here! How can there be nothing in any of these houses? Not a scrap of food or a single round."

"Somebody's been here," Connor said, "and cleaned the whole place out."

"No shit, Sherlock!" James said.

"Don't get pissed at me. We both knew this was a long shot."

James sighed. "I'm sorry. I just don't know how we're gonna do this. How the hell are we supposed to go up against that many and come out alive? It's just gonna get us all killed."

"It might, but I'd rather die fighting than surrender."

"You're just full of motivation tonight aren't you?"

"Somebody has to be. Usually, my big brother is, but he's having a tough time right now. So I'm stepping up on the inspirational speeches."

James shook his head and stared at the shelf he'd knocked over.

Connor was worried for his brother. This whole thing with finding the group and taking on the responsibility of leadership was eating away at James, especially when things went wrong—as they inevitably did. Connor was trying to help his brother find his way through all this.

How do you do that when you, yourself are lost? Connor thought.

Connor had never reconciled with the fact that God had let their parents die. Yes, he knew God hadn't caused their deaths, but they were dead now. Nothing could change that. Bad things *did* happen, whether to good or bad people. That was just part of life. But the pill was easier to swallow when it wasn't your own parents who'd been brutally murdered. He had all this anger inside of him, with regrets and guilt piled on top. Would those feelings ever go away? Or would they be what finally broke him, like it was breaking his brother?

"Let's go," James said, walking back through the door and into the house.

Connor followed. How had they even gotten themselves into this situation? One day, they'd been on the ranch in Montana with not a care in the world. The next, they were fighting for their lives in a race to save their parents. They'd failed miserably at that. Then they'd rescued Emmett, Alexis, and Ana, and things had begun to look up. But that had only lasted for a day and then their naïve sense of wonder gave way to the harsh reality of the world. Now here they were, searching for a few rounds or guns that wouldn't even make a bit of difference against what they faced. Were they willing to risk their lives, everything they had left, for strangers? He almost wished they could just leave them, continue north to Alaska, set up at their wilderness camp, and make a life for themselves. But he knew in his heart that wasn't an option, no matter how much he might want it. They could never run from something like this. It was in his nature to fight to his last breath, so that's what he'd do.

As they walked outside to the waiting Hummer, Connor randomly wondered if Squeezer was still alive. He may be just a snake, but he'd helped him through a tough time. Shaking his head, he climbed into the passenger seat. It didn't matter now.

"Nothin'?" Tank asked.

"Nope," James said.

"Damn Reclaimers," Tank said. "Those bastards got to it before us. They probably scavenged everything for miles."

"We're just wasting time," Connor said.

"I know," James said. "Maybe we should turn ourselves over."

"You know it won't do a damn bit 'a good," Tank said.

"I know," James said. "But maybe there's a chance—"

"What chance?" Connor asked, cutting him off. "That the psychopath who's randomly killing everybody will suddenly decide to be lenient? What kind of fantasy world are you living in? They'll kill us *and* the rest of our group."

"Then what do we do?" James asked, throwing his hands up.

"Simple," Tank said, "we fight till we can't fight no more."

"Why are you so adamant about helping them?" Chloe asked Tank and then looked at Connor and James. "I'm not saying we should leave them, but we barely know them."

Tank shrugged. "At this point, we've all killed people. The only thing that's separating us from them, from being murderers, is that we kill to protect. If we leave them, are we really any better than the bad guys? What has all our killing and surviving been for if we leave their friends to die?"

Everyone was silent. *Were* they any different from those people, like Tank said? What made them any better? Did they really kill to protect, or just to survive? Who got to decide who lived and died anyway? Did they even have a say in the matter, or were they all just pieces on a board, moved against their will?

Oh, stop it! Connor thought.

"We should get movin'," Connor said.

"Right," Tank said, "where to now? We can't do much scouting in the dark."

"I guess we continue to look until just before the sun comes up," James said. "There are all those subdivisions closer to town."

"That sounds extremely dangerous," Chloe said. "You sure you guys need more ammunition and guns?"

"Yeah," James said, "we both have less than three magazines for our ARs and the handguns won't do much good if it turns into an all-out gunfight."

"Closer to town it is, then," Tank said, turning the Hummer around and heading back the way they'd come.

"We need to be ready to get out quick," James said.

"I'll be ready," Tank said. "I hate not being able to go in with you guys, but for now I think it's better that I stay out here in case you guys need to catch a ride quickly."

Tank drove them back to US-14 and headed toward Sheridan. In less than a mile, they'd arrived at the first road leading south. With the half-moon lighting the darkness, they could make out the shapes of houses in the night.

"This is it," James said.

"We either find some weapons in these houses," Connor said, "or we go in as is. In a couple of hours, the sun will be up and so will our time."

Tank pulled to a stop at the first house and Connor jumped out, sweeping the darkness with the flashlight attached to his handgun. The beam had dimmed since they'd started searching a few hours earlier. He would need to change the batteries soon.

James climbed out of the backseat, wincing as his feet hit the ground.

His side must be bothering him still, Connor thought.

They'd need to change their bandages when they had some down-time, if they ever *had* any downtime. Looking at his brother, he could see James setting his jaw. The fight hadn't left him yet. No, his brother was far from giving up, and Connor felt bad for thinking James was breaking. He'd been knocked down and was trying to stand up again. Connor just needed to offer him a helping hand.

"You ready, brother?" Connor asked.

James looked him in the eyes. "Let's do it."

"I really wish we still had Google," Chloe said. "Then, we could just find the nearest gun store and go there."

Tank chuckled. "If only it were that easy."

He looked down at his watch.

C'mon guys, Tank thought, *where the hell are you?*

"You think something's wrong?" Chloe asked. "They've been in there awhile."

"Thirty minutes isn't that long," Tank said, trying to mask his own concern. "They could've found something. Or the house has a basement."

"You think we should help?"

"That's not the plan. If they came out a different way and we missed 'em, it could lead to disaster. And we're missing the firepower they have with those rifles. All I have is my handgun."

"Oh, I didn't think about that."

"And maybe they went ahead to the next house."

Chloe nodded.

He wished he believed that. The fact was, he was a lot more worried than he'd let on. They should've been back long before now. It didn't take that long to check a small house like the one they were in. Tank hadn't heard a gunshot or seen the flashlight beams going outside. They could've slipped out, but why? He'd turned the Hummer off awhile ago and now they sat in complete darkness. With his eyes adjusted to the dim moonlight outside, he could see just enough to make out shapes and movement in the darkness. But it was also dark enough that sometimes that movement was more in his mind than outside.

Something smacked against the back window and Chloe screamed. Tank pulled out his handgun, pointing it at the window. There was a face beyond the glass. He recognized it. Turning the key on enough to get power but without turning on the headlights or dome lights, he rolled the window down.

"Son of a bitch!" Tank exclaimed. "I almost shot you."

"Sorry about that," James said, smiling ruefully as he came around to Tank's window. "Can you unlock the back? We need to load some guns."

"You found some?" Chloe asked, still trying to calm her breathing.

"Yeah, a whole closet full! Three rifles, two shotguns, and four handguns, along with a few hundred rounds of ammo for each."

"Nice," Tank said, pressing the door lock, "Rear door's unlocked."

"Thanks, bro," James said as he disappeared around the back of the Hummer.

Tank holstered his handgun, flipping the safety back on. He could just make out Connor in the darkness behind James, hauling a couple of boxes. So they'd found some guns. Good. Maybe they would stand a fighting chance after all.

After another trip inside, the brothers climbed back into the Hummer.

"Next house," James said, pointing down the street.

"I ain't your damn chauffeur!" Tank said.

"But you are good, sir," James said.

"Don't make me punch you," Tank said.

"Why'd you guys have your flashlights off back there?" Chloe asked.

"A couple of zombies were fenced inside the backyard," James said. "Didn't want to have them get all frenzied with the lights."

"That," Connor said, "and the batteries in James's light died."

"And that," James said, confirming Connor's comment. "We should be able to find a few AAs in the next house. Tank, you have a light I can borrow?"

"Sure," Tank said, pulling to a stop in front of the next house. "But you can't use it."

"What?"

"Nope, not without knowing the password."

"Password?" James asked. "Is it 'Tank rules'?"

"Nope."

"'Tank is a badass'?"

"Nope."

"Just give him the damn light," Connor said.

"He has to earn the light," Tank said.

"'Tank sucks,'" James said.

"You're not even close."

"Boys, you realize we're in a hurry, right?" Chloe asked.

Tank looked at James. He wasn't even close. It would take him all night to figure it out.

"Lil' Jamesy Boy," Tank said, opening up his glove box. "That is the password."

"Dude, c'mon," James said, taking the flashlight.

"What?" Tank asked, smiling. "Makes a damn good password."

"You suck," James said, smiling slightly.

He climbed out of the Hummer and Connor followed, shaking his head.

"We'll be back in a few," Connor said.

"Don't get lost like last time," Tank said.

Connor shut the door and the brothers moved off into the darkness. James swung his AR to his side and drew his tomahawk to use with the flashlight Tank had given him. Connor was right next to him, handgun ready. They arrived at the front door and posted up. A nod and they were breaching the house, their lights disappearing inside.

"Just when I begin to think you're not a child, you prove me wrong," Chloe said, shaking her head.

"What?" Tank asked. "The password thing?"

"Of course," Chloe said. "We only have a couple hours left before the Reclaimers kill someone, and here you are making James have to guess a password to give him a flashlight so he doesn't get killed in the dark."

"I'm just an asshole."

"I don't think that's true. An asshole wouldn't be willing to sacrifice himself to save people he doesn't even know. He wouldn't be a hundred percent loyal to his friends. And he wouldn't be cracking jokes to lighten the mood when his friends are having a tough time. I've known plenty of them, and I don't think you're one."

"Maybe I'm just an asshole that cares."

"Yeah, or maybe you pretend to be one to cover up who you truly are."

"Where the hell is this comin' from?" Tank asked, glancing back at her. Her brunette hair was pulled into a bun and her pouty lips didn't look half bad when she wasn't scowling. Actually, she was kind of hot when she wasn't being a total beeyotch. "I thought you hated me? Called me a dick, asshole, pig... Am I missing anything?"

"I thought you were," Chloe said, "but I talked to James. He said I was wrong about you."

"That little—" Tank said, "I wouldn't trust anything he says."

"It got me thinking. Maybe I should give you another chance."

"Sorry to disappoint you, honey. I *am* an asshole. I just happen to have some good friends."

"There's more to you. I can see that now."

"Well, you just got me all figured out now, don't ya?"

"I'm pretty good at reading people."

"Well, think what you will. I stand by it."

"That's fine. I know better."

"Whatever," Tank said.

How much truth was there to that? He didn't hate people as much as he put on, but he didn't really like them either. And he did care more than he showed, but he didn't care that much. At least, he didn't think he did. There were those he did care about, and for them he'd take on the entire world. Others? Nah. But maybe he did care more than he realized. That was scary to admit. Letting people get close usually just ended in pain. He'd learned a long time ago, after his parents' divorce, that it was a lot easier to keep people at a distance. It was the people he let get close that hurt him the most.

The brothers returned a few minutes later, having found a little bit of food and some batteries. They stashed the food in the back. James and Connor installed the new batteries in their flashlights, then James handed Tank's light back. They moved on to the next house and repeated the process. As the night turned into early morning, they searched on, trying desperately to find something that would turn the tide. They acquired another gun and a little more ammunition, but they still didn't know if it would be enough. It wasn't firepower they were lacking now, it was manpower. They were only three versus the Reclaimers'—what, three dozen? Four dozen?

As the hours passed, Tank began to realize something: They couldn't win this fight and they all knew it. They searched anyway. Moving from house to house, they checked the whole subdivision. After the last stop, James and Connor climbed into the Hummer, a somber mood hanging in the air.

"That's it," James said. "We've done everything we can."

"Do you think you're prepared?" Chloe asked.

"No," Connor said, "but it's the best we can do."

"Isn't it a little weird that we haven't seen a single undead?" Tank asked.

"I was just thinking about that a few houses ago," James said.

"The Reclaimers must've cleared them out," Connor said. "Either that or something drew them into town."

"You mean like a gas station exploding?" Tank asked, smiling.

"Yeah, that probably did it," James said.

"It'll be light soon," Connor said.

"We better head towards the Reclaimers and scout it out," James said.

"Time to go," Tank said, pulling the Hummer back out onto US-14. The headlights shone in the darkness as light began to peek over the horizon.

5

A NEW HOPE

Alexis heard a gunshot echo outside the barn and closed her eyes. Tears wet her cheeks. They'd taken Ana and then Mila. Jezz was going to kill them both—had already killed one. Who would be next? Her? Where were her dad and the children? Where were James and Connor? She was worried about them, especially James. The peace she'd felt the night before had shattered the instant Jezz had walked into the barn that morning. Her whole demeanor had changed, like she was a predator searching for prey. Gone was the friendly woman who'd first talked to Alexis.

She waited for the second gunshot, but it never came. Why had there only been one? Her mind summoned images of all the things Jezz could be doing to torture them, but there was nothing she could do about it. She would be next. A sob escaped her.

She was trying to be strong, but everything seemed so hopeless. Her last friend in this world was dead, her dad was missing—probably dead, too—James and Connor were lost, and she was captive to an insane person, again. When her dad had saved her from her mother's house at the start of all this, she'd thought the worst thing they were going to face were the infected. That was far from the truth. The people they kept running into—they were worse. They were the ones who would end up killing them. She began to panic. How were they going to get out of this?

Remember last night, said a small voice in the back of her mind.

Last night. When she'd come to the end of her wits, she'd prayed. And God *had* answered her, then and there. She'd heard Him speak to her. Well, she'd heard a voice in her head, which could mean she was going insane, joining the rest of the people in this messed-up world. But the peace she'd felt in the midst of everything—how did she explain that? She'd chosen to believe then. Did she still believe, now? It'd only been one night, but everything had changed since then. She'd lost so much; could she bear to lose more? What did she have to lose now if her dad and Ana were both dead? She had her own life, the lives of the children, and everyone else in the barn. Maybe when Jezz came back she could convince her to let them all go.

No, that wouldn't work. Maybe she could do something else—get her to spare the children, or just make a difference some-how. Even if she didn't have a reason to live, she could still try and save the others. She would stay strong and fight for them. Alexis took a deep, calming breath and wiped the tears off on her shoulders as best as she could with her hands chained behind her back. Looking around the room, she set her jaw. So many of them looked broken, like they'd already given up, but hadn't she looked that way a second ago? Maybe, but for now she held onto hope—a hope that they might survive this, or at least some of them. If she could just help save one, her death would mean something.

The minutes ticked by and the peace from the night before returned to her—not all at once like a flood but as a gradual trickle of water. Before she knew it, she was calm. The world was in chaos around her, but it didn't have to be that way inside her.

"She's going to kill us all, isn't she?" a woman to her left asked.

Alexis glanced over, recognizing the dyed blonde hair and face. The last time she'd talked to this woman, she'd had determination in her eyes and a friendly smile on her lips. Beverly—the woman she'd helped pick out a rifle before Chugwater.

"I don't know," Alexis answered, trying to display a sense of peace. She might feel peaceful, but she didn't know how to show that to those around her.

"She is. I know she is," Beverly said.

"Maybe," Alexis said, "we can't change that. We *can* change how we spend our last moments, though."

"What the hell do you mean?" said the big man with tattoos to her left. Greg. "How can we spend this time any differently when we're chained up like animals ready for slaughter?"

"Our bodies may be chained, but—"

"Cut the crap, lady," Greg broke in. "We're dead, whether we want to be or not. I just know I'm not going down without a fight. If I get a chance, I'll kill that crazy bitch."

"We can make the best of this situation," Alexis reiterated. "We can't give up or we might as well be dead already."

"We should be," said one of the men. He wore a tattered blue t-shirt and his long brown hair was matted with dirt and blood.

"But we aren't," Alexis said. "And there's a reason for that."

She looked over at Beverly and gave her a smile. Craning her neck, she looked at those around her. Most of them were looking up at her now that she'd begun to speak. Expressions ranging from anger to sadness, and defeat to hope adorned their faces. She could do this. Helping them through this situation would be what she lived for. Whether it was only a few more hours or a couple of days, she didn't know. But she wouldn't give up. She would be a beacon of hope for those around her. That's exactly what she'd been called to do.

"We don't have to be hopeless," Alexis said, raising her voice so those around her could hear. "Just because we're captives doesn't mean we're defeated."

"No, we're not defeated, but to be all positive is like blowing rainbows up our asses!" Greg said.

"Why do you fight it, Greg?" Alexis asked him. "If you want to wallow in your despair, then do so, but don't drag these people down with you. Just look at some of the heroes from history who were in captivity but not defeated: the Apostle Paul, Dietrich Bonhoeffer,

Anne Frank, Jesus. All these people were killed because of what they believed or who they were, and their legacies have lasted for centuries. If we all die today, our deaths will be the end of these bodies, but they could be the beginning of something else."

"Pretty speech," Greg said, smirking. "I feel much better now, thanks." He seemed like he wanted to say more. Instead, he looked her in the eyes. She could tell his rage was just below the surface, but he held it back.

"What should we do, then?" asked a woman with highlights in her hair.

"Live each moment as if it was our last," Alexis said, "which it very well might be."

"Yes, but how do we actually *do* that?" Beverly asked.

"By remembering our lives and those we've loved, sharing in this captivity together instead of alone. Beverly, what's your most cherished memory?"

Beverly lowered her head like she was about to cry. Alexis let her feel the pain of that moment, hoping she would be able to move past it and embrace the beauty and joy of remembrance. Beverly looked up with tears in her eyes but a smile on her face.

"The day my daughter was born," Beverly said. "She was the most beautiful thing I'd ever seen. As I held her in my arms, I thought to myself that this moment would never be surpassed. It wasn't." By the end, her tears had slowed and her smile had grown.

"Where's your daughter now?" Alexis asked.

"She's dead," Beverly said.

"I'm sorry," Alexis said.

"It's okay. It happened three years ago. Leukemia. That first year after I lost her was hard—a lot harder than this, actually."

"We were born facing hardships," Alexis said, "and we will die before we stop facing them. We just have to remember to stay strong and keep our faith."

Beverly nodded. "You're right."

"What if we don't go anywhere when we die?" a man asked from her left.

Alexis glanced over at him. He was a younger man with red hair and a full beard. She'd never met him before, though she'd seen him around.

"What's your name?" Alexis asked.

"Troy," said the man.

"Well, Troy. What do you believe in?"

"I was raised Catholic, but it didn't stick."

"Me too," said an older woman with black hair. When Alexis looked at her, she added. "I'm Abby."

"I can't tell you what to believe in. You have to decide that for yourselves. But I can tell you what I believe: there is a God and he died for our sins." That felt weird for her to say. She hadn't talked about this kind of stuff since she was young. It was almost an alien concept to her, even though she believed it whole-heartedly now. The words just flowed out of her and she continued. "I was raised a Christian but didn't embrace it as an adult until... yesterday."

A few of the group laughed and she smiled. She was breaking through their walls, getting them to open up. Now she just had to keep them talking and show them that they could truly *live* in these last moments.

"What about you?" Beverly asked. "What's your memory?"

The question took Alexis aback, but she should've been prepared to share her past if she was asking these people to dig into theirs. The memory was easy to recall, but it brought such pain that she rarely thought about it. It was her little brother, who'd been taken too soon.

"My little brother's face when we used to build with Legos in his room. He always thought it was so cool when his big sister would play with him. I just did it to see that smile on his face."

She paused, remembering those times. It'd been so long ago, but the image was burned into her mind. The last time she'd seen her brother's smile, Mason had been on the back of her dad's ATV as they drove down the two-track on their ranch in Texas. Dad had finally started letting her drive the miniature ATV when they went out riding. Mom hated it, saying a ten-year-old was too young to drive anything. They'd been out behind the house and Mason held onto Emmett in front of him, smiling back at her. He stuck out his tongue and she laughed, sticking her tongue out in return. They were approaching The Hill, which was the best part of the whole ride. At the time it had seemed like a mountain, but once she'd grown up she'd realized it was just a big hill.

"Something happened to him," Beverly said, snapping her back to the present.

Alexis looked up at her, unaware of the tears gathering in her eyes. She nodded, swallowing the lump in her throat.

"He died in an ATV accident when we were young. It was the cause of my parents' divorce," Alexis said, still lost in the memory.

Just thinking about his smile brought everything back: her dad's ATV flipping over; Mason tumbling down the hill; the ATV landing squarely on him, crushing his chest; the ride to the emergency room; her feelings of being completely helpless; the funeral and the rift it had caused in her parent's marriage. Looking back, she could see that the rift had been there years before, but the death of her brother had ripped it wide open. She remembered the yelling late at night, her hiding under the covers, crying, and her dad coming in to slump against her bed, his head in his hands.

Then the next hit had come—the divorce. In the same year her brother had passed away, her parents split up. The only reason Jane had won custody of Alexis was because she accused Emmett of negligent care, and she'd planned the court hearing while he was deployed overseas. Alexis never forgave her mother for that and she knew it. When Jane had married George, she'd become even more distant and embittered toward Alexis and Emmett. It was a shame. They had once been a happy family, but Jane couldn't handle all the time Emmett was away.

"I lost my brother and my family split apart in the same year," Alexis said, looking around at them. "We were never the same after that. It wasn't until my dad was out of the service and I was in high school that we reconnected. But I would rather keep those memories of my brother's smile, even if all the pain comes with it."

Beverly nodded. "The pain doesn't dull the joy."

"No, it doesn't," Alexis said. She glanced at the man with the ragged blue t-shirt who'd spoken before. "What's your name?"

"Evan," said the man.

"And your best memory?" Alexis asked.

"Stephanie's birthday," Evan said after taking a few moments to think. "We were all there—my wife and four daughters. Just the six of us. After the party ended, we were all lying on the trampoline, looking up at the clouds and guessing what they were... It was perfect." There were tears in his eyes. The small smile on his face faded quickly, replaced by pain and anger. "That was Friday. The next day I was at the school when we got the broadcast to stay where we were. I listened. After two days of sitting there, I couldn't take it any longer. I went back to our house. They... were all dead. My whole life torn away in a single day."

"I'm sorry. You're not alone in your loss," Alexis said.

"I just want my girls back," Evan said, choking back tears.

"I'm sorry, man," said a younger man. "I know how much you loved your family. We're here for you. You don't have to face this alone."

"Thanks, Lucas," Evan said, closing his eyes. Tears ran down his cheeks and he leaned back against the post.

"I was lucky," Lucas said, looking at Alexis. "I don't have a family. For once, being an orphan has paid off. My best memory would be when you guys got us out of the school. I thought we were going to die in that gym. Then you showed up and saved us. I can't thank you enough for that."

"Yeah, saved us just to die out here," Greg said. "So much better."

"Look, Greg," Lucas said. "I know you've had it rough, but man up! At least out here we have a fighting chance instead of sitting back there, waiting to die."

"You little prick, you have no idea what I've been through," Greg said, growling.

"Stop it, you two!" said an older woman with gray hair. She looked at Alexis, smiling. "Hi, I'm Helen, the third-grade teacher. I appreciate what you're doing here. It's good to remember that there's still hope."

Alexis smiled. "Thanks."

"Now, my memory is a long one," Helen began, "but I think we have time."

A few of them laughed. Helen had that old-woman charisma about her. After she'd finished sharing her story, people started following her lead, and they spent the next few hours sharing their best memories. There were tears, laughs, and intimate moments shared between them all. Only two didn't share. Greg passed and Margaret wouldn't even look up when addressed. As people began to quiet down, Alexis found her mind wandering back to what was going on outside. Were James and Connor even coming for them? Where was her dad? Was he still alive? The questions weighed down on her.

The morning turned to afternoon. A few people were able to nap, but most of them just sat chained to the posts, their minds wandering. The uplifting mood faded as the hours passed but it didn't feel as hopeless as it had before. There was a reason these people were still alive: they were survivors. It would take a lot more than this to completely break them. Well, except for Margaret. She hadn't spoken since that morning and spent most of the time staring at the ground or crying.

The pole barn stayed surprisingly cool during the heat of the day, even though the sun was beating down outside. She was thankful for that because nobody had brought them any food or water throughout the day. In fact, they hadn't heard anything around the barn since the gunshot that morning.

She shifted her weight, as she'd been doing often. Every muscle in her body ached and her throat felt like she'd swallowed sand. She'd never felt this restless before. It was like sitting on an airplane for an entire day but all the while with her arms pinned behind her back. But as the exhaustion of the last couple of days and the emotional strain of being held captive settled on her, she closed her eyes and leaned her head back against the pole. Finally, she fell into a fitful sleep.

6

IMPLICATIONS

J ames sat in the backseat of the Hummer as Tank drove them south on US-14 toward the location of the 'X' on the map, which was scrawled on the back of the note. They'd figured out where to go by comparing the crudely drawn map with the road atlas. Now, they were on their way to some back road that cut off of US-14 and headed east. The Reclaimer's hideout was somewhere south of that road, but they weren't sure exactly where. They needed to find somewhere high to scout, which shouldn't be difficult because the country around Sheridan was covered in hills.

Virus by Memphis May Fire played through the speakers on Tank's iPod. James closed his eyes. It felt good just to sit there, listening to the lyrics. It almost made things seem normal, aside from the throbbing in his ear and side, the pressing weight of his tactical vest, the AR-15 on his lap, and the guilt sitting heavy in his mind. Other than all that, it was almost normal. Okay, so none of it was normal and he felt stupid for even thinking it. He was glad Memphis had released this song right before things went down the drain; otherwise, they would've missed out on a great addition to their *Apocalypse Road Trip playlist v2*. His iPod was still in his truck, and he hoped it was okay. He'd really miss his music if it wasn't. Then again, it wouldn't be the end of the world. Wait. Actually, it would be.

He smiled and then felt bad for smiling. What the hell was going on with him? It was as if his mind and emotions were inside a pinball machine. Taking a deep breath, he let it out slowly. His control was slipping, and he could feel it. That was what happened with his episodes—he lost what little control he had. What would happen if he had an episode in the middle of combat? It'd almost gotten him bitten before. Would this be what got him or someone else killed? No, he wouldn't let that happen. He could keep his mind under control. Or could he?

Lord, help me, James prayed, in desperation.

He wanted to say more, but that's all that came to mind. Everything just seemed to be going wrong and he had no idea how to fix any of it. His faith felt strong one moment, like he could move mountains; then, with a new turn of events, he was right back where he'd started. When was it ever going to end?

When you let go and trust, a small part of his mind said.

Let go and trust.

That was something he had an extremely difficult time doing. Even in normal life, before the apocalypse, he'd had a hard time with that. He wanted to have control, to be the one making the plans and in charge, but things very rarely worked out when he took the reins from God. He usually ended up in the ditch, a wreck of emotions. It just never worked out for him when he grasped for the control he knew he didn't have. If he thought back, he could remember all the times when he'd released control. Everything had worked out wonderfully—perhaps not exactly how he'd wanted it, but usually the situations had ended up better than he would have imagined. So why was it so hard for him to let go?

The Hummer slowed and James opened his eyes. Tank turned left onto a red dirt road leading east into the hills.

"We need to be careful," James said, adjusting the bandage over his ear. "The map may not be the most accurate."

"My thoughts precisely," Tank said. "The first place that looks good, I'll pull over."

They continued at a much slower speed. The sky before them was brightening quickly. There would be enough light to see soon. That meant they only had about thirty minutes until sunrise and the first death. James tried not to think about who they would kill first, but it was useless. His mind kept bringing up images of Alexis or little Olive. Hopefully, it would be one of the other survivors from Burns, just not Mila, Olive, or the kids. He felt sick to his stomach for wishing death on anyone, but he couldn't lose someone else he cared about. He could barely hold it together as it was.

Tank turned the headlights off since it was now bright enough to see. They drove up the first hill on the dirt road and noticed a gated drive leading up the hill to their left. It looked like it would lead to the top of the hill and was the highest location in the area.

"This looks promising," Tank said, slowing to a stop.

"I'll check the gate," Connor said, getting out.

"Hopefully we can see the Reclaimer's hideout from here," James said.

"Yeah, otherwise we may have to just go in guns blazin'," Tank said.

"It may come to that," James said. "Let's call that our plan C."

"What about plan B?" Chloe asked.

"Find another hill farther east and hope it doesn't land us right on top of them," James said.

"What if none of the plans work?" Chloe asked.

"Then..." James started to say but finished the thought in his head. *We turn ourselves in and hope for the best.* "We come up with another plan."

"We have a whole alphabet full of plans to run through," Tank said.

Connor swung the old metal gate open and motioned them forward. Tank drove through and Connor closed the gate and then hopped back in.

"It was dummy-locked," Connor said, rolling down his window and resting his AR on the mirror.

"Smart," Tank said, as he started up the road.

"Dummy-locked?" Chloe asked. "You mean it was made to look like it was locked when it really wasn't?"

"Exactly," James said, rolling down his window.

"Be ready," Connor said. "It looked like fresh vehicle tracks leading up here."

"What kind of vehicle?" Tank asked. "How much did it weigh? How many in the pack?"

"What?" Chloe asked.

"He's a hunter," Tank said. "He knows how to track."

"Possibly three different vehicles," Connor said, "one with some aggressive tread."

Chloe looked at him skeptically.

"You can tell basic stuff like that," James said. "Common sense."

"I never learned to track vehicles," Chloe said with a chuckle.

"It's an acquired skill," James said, smiling.

The conversation died as they rounded a bend in the road and began the final ascent to the top of the hill. When they crested it, Tank brought the Hummer to a stop.

"Damn!" Tank said.

The whole top of the hill had been flattened and a spot the size of a football field had been cleared, with a seven-foot-tall berm around the clearing. The exposed dirt and rock were red. More than likely, it was the same gravel used on the road. Set up on the east side of the gravel pit were three large, white, pavilion-style tents. On the west, just south of where they sat, was a line of three black vehicles with tinted windows—two SUVs and a vehicle that looked like a Hummer crossed with an armored truck. On the north end of the clearing was a crashed Black Hawk helicopter.

"What the hell?" James said. "What is this?"

"Government," Tank said. "Has to be."

"Military, judging from the chopper," Connor said.

"But why are there no insignias on the vehicles?" James asked, pointing at the SUV.

"Must be black ops or something covert," Connor said.

"Well, hot damn!" Tank exclaimed. "This might be our lucky day. They're bound to have some good gear! Like that beefy thing over there," he said and pointed to the vehicle at the end.

"Let's go, then," James said.

Tank pulled over to the last vehicle in the line, passing all three pavilions. As they passed, the walls blew in the wind, giving James a brief look inside the last pavilion. Everything was strewn about the tent and he didn't see a single person. Something bad had happened here. Tank stopped the Hummer.

"I'm going to go check that thing out!" Tank said as he got out, followed by James and Connor.

"Just stay close to the Hummer in case we need to get out fast," James said, walking over to join his brother, who was facing the closest pavilion.

"No shit," Tank responded, walking over to the vehicle. "We'll be able to see someone comin' from a long way off."

"I'll just stay in here," Chloe said from inside the Hummer.

"Good girl," Tank said. "Oh man, this thing is badass!"

"I'm just going to ignore that," Chloe said.

"Ready?" James asked his brother.

Connor nodded and they moved toward the pavilion. James arrived first and parted the fabric of the entrance to look inside. There were computer terminals, random technological devices, and tables with paperwork scattered on them. This would be the work station. Most of the tables had been tipped onto their sides and everything was thrown about the room. Either people had left in a hurry or a tornado had come through here. Or something worse.

"This is just like in all the movies," James said.

"I hate to agree with a comment like that," Connor said, "but I think you're right."

"Tank, come check this out," James called out.

"One second," Tank called from the far side of the Hummer, twenty yards away.

"What do you think they were doing here?" James asked.

"Something to do with the outbreak, that's for sure," Connor said. "No way this is a coincidence."

"What'd you guys...?" Tank asked, walking into the pavilion. "No way! This is just like—"

"In all the movies," Connor finished for him.

"We know," James said.

"This isn't good," Tank said.

"Why?" James asked.

"In most of those movies, it meant the government was somehow involved when they found something like this."

"You don't think..." Connor said.

"Yeah, I'm considerin' it," Tank said. "There might be a whole lot more to this than we've even begun to realize."

"I wish we had time to see what information we could find," James said.

"Maybe after we rescue all your homies, we can come back," Tank said.

"How's that armored-vehicle thing out there?" Connor asked.

"Locked," Tank said. "It's called a Gurkha LAPV, at least that's what it had on the back door. It looks like an armored Hummer, and I want it!"

"Okay," James said, planning, "Tank, look around here for the keys and stay close to the Hummer, just in case. Connor, go check whether you can see the Reclaimer's hideout from the berm. I'll go check the other two pavilions."

"Roger," Connor said, leaving the pavilion.

"Got it, Jamesy Boy," Tank said, going over to the closest table with paperwork and miscellaneous items scattered around.

James exited and looked around. It was light enough to see now, which was good for scouting, but it meant they had maybe twenty minutes. It was time to kick it into a higher gear. He jogged over to the second pavilion, keeping a sharp eye out as he did. This place looked completely abandoned. If there were any zombies around, the noise from the Hummer would've drawn them out. Plus, he could see the whole border of the gravel pit easily. They should have nothing to worry about.

He kept his guard up anyway.

Arriving at the second pavilion, he eased inside the flap. The contents of this one were different than the last. Crates of supplies were scattered around the pavilion—MREs, water, empty ammunition cans, and other miscellaneous items. Most of the crates were still upright, but a few were tipped over, the contents spilled on the ground. There was still a good amount of non-perishable food supplies and water here. That would be useful. It seemed like most of the ammunition cans were empty, though. Quickly, but carefully, he searched the entire place, finding nothing that would aid them immediately.

Moving outside, he made his way to the last pavilion. The side of this one had a vertical slash the length of the wall, and James entered through it. This had been the bunk room. Twenty cots stood in rigid order around the tent, and belongings, gear, and guns were sitting neatly on the bunks. This one couldn't have been any more different than the other two. It looked untouched. No, even stranger, it was completely organized. Everything had a home and not a single item was out of place. The white walls looked like they'd been stained at some point, but they were clean now. In the back corner of the tent, a small, square room had been sectioned off with the same white fabric the rest of the tent was made of.

James approached the room. How had this pavilion been spared from being ransacked like the other two? It wasn't as if nothing in here was useful. He caught sight of multiple untouched pairs of military gear, tactical vests, plate carriers, and even firearms on the bunks. Each one almost looked like a memorial to the people who'd used them. Nametags showed on uniforms, which were neatly folded and laying near the ends of the bunks. He paused by one on the way to the sectioned-off room. The name tag had a drop of blood on it. Romeo. Picking up the uniform with his off hand, he took a closer look. The thing smelled horrible, and now that it was unfolded, he could see that blood covered the rest of it.

"What the..." James said, tossing the rancid-smelling garment aside.

There was a sudden movement by the sectioned-off part of the tent, and James reacted before his mind fully processed it. He raised his AR at the man now standing there.

"Don't move or I blow your face off!" the man shouted.

He had a black combat rifle aimed at James's head. The man was outfitted in full Kryptek tactical gear, with a plate carrier and helmet with NVGs, and had the drop on him. James still had another few inches to raise his AR to get a shot, but one look into the man's crazed, bloodshot eyes stopped him.

Connor climbed the berm surrounding the gravel pit to the south. Nearing the top, he dropped to a crouch and proceeded with caution, careful not to skyline. The rise and fall of the landscape continued on for miles—deep cuts, punctuated by hills and ridges. Small trees grew in the bottoms of the cuts where water collected, while the hillsides and ridges were covered in patches of sagebrush. The road continued down the other side of the hill they were on, dropping into a small valley and then continuing up the next hill, snaking eastward. In the bottom of the valley, a driveway split off south until it disappeared behind another hill to the southeast. He couldn't see the Reclaimers' hideout, but that was a good thing because he now knew where the hideout would be. If the map was correct, it was down that driveway, south of the road they were on.

It would be easy to hide in this country. They could stick to the cuts, follow those toward where the hideout was, and then crawl up the ridges to get the lay of the land beyond. They could scout the hideout without the Reclaimers ever knowing they were there. Finally, something they could work with.

Connor turned around. They would need to hurry. They had a small hike ahead of them to get to the ridge where they'd be able to see the hideout. He picked his way down the berm, stopping at the bottom. Glancing at the far pavilion, he raised his AR to his shoulder in a split second, aiming through the scope at the man who held James hostage. Connor cursed.

"Don't even think about it!" yelled the man. "You both have till the count of three to drop your weapons before I kill him! One!"

James was almost a hundred yards away, with his own handgun being held to his head. The man was well outfitted and looked like he knew what he was doing. He never let more than just one eye show around the side of his brother's head. To make matters worse, the man kept switching which side of James's head he was looking around, which made it almost impossible for Connor to make the shot off hand at this distance.

"Two!"

Tank came out of the pavilion, his hands in the air. If Connor could just get prone and take the shot from a stable position, he might be able to pull it off. But if he missed by just half an inch, he would shoot his brother in the head. Just half an inch. Was he that confident in his shooting? With enough time, a good rest, and a stationary target, yes. He was confident he could make that shot, but this shot with his brother's life on the line? Connor stood there, breathing as steadily as possible, and still the reticle of his optic wavered between the man's head and his brother's.

"Three!"

7

BETRAYAL

A lexis woke up, yawning. The first thing she noticed was that it was considerably darker in the barn now, so she must've slept for a few hours. That was good; she needed it. She tried to stretch, but her hands were chained behind her back. Wait, it was dark out? She took in her surroundings, awareness coming fully back to her. She was chained to a pole, a prisoner of the Reclaimers. It was late in the afternoon now, maybe even early evening. Jezz would be back soon.

The thought brought fear rising to her throat like bile, but she swallowed it down. It wouldn't be very appropriate if she spent the whole morning motivating them and lifting their spirits just to have fear disable her. A few deep breaths later, she'd calmed considerably. Most of the survivors were awake and seemed somewhat positive. The whole feel of the barn had changed in just a few hours. They were still in the same place they'd been before, but their attitudes had shifted—most of them anyway.

Voices drifted to her through the outside door, and she braced herself as it opened.

Alexis's mind couldn't grasp what she saw. She just stared, unable to comprehend.

Ana walked through the door, unchained, and with a handgun in her hand. Jezz walked in behind her.

"Hello, my dears," Jezz purred, standing tall before them. Ana stood just behind her.

"Wh...What?" Alexis croaked out, finding her voice.

Jezz looked over at her, her smile spreading.

"Whatever is the matter, dear?" she asked.

Alexis stared at Ana, but Ana didn't so much as glance down at her, as she kept her eyes straight ahead. How was she still alive, and why was she unchained? Was she still a prisoner? And why did she have a *gun*? The handgun Ana held was missing the magazine. It would only have one round in the chamber.

"Oh, I see you noticed my newest assistant," Jezz said, stepping aside to give Alexis a better look at Ana. Still, Ana didn't look at her and Alexis didn't know what to think or feel. Her chest was a swirl of emotions and her mind a jumble of thoughts.

"Ana?" Alexis asked.

Ana didn't respond. She didn't even move.

"Yes, that is her name, and you are Alexis," Jezz said. "Now that introductions are over, we can move on to business. We have been waiting patiently all day for our guests to arrive, but it seems like they have decided not to show up to our party—again. That leaves me with a conundrum. I have a whole bunch of other guests ready to start the party and yet we are waiting on only a few. I have to ask, should we start without them?"

Alexis didn't take her eyes off Ana until that moment. What did she mean "start the party?" She was afraid she knew the answer to that.

"They'll show up," Alexis said, desperately. "There's no need to rush the party. We aren't going anywhere."

Jezz looked down at her, contemplating. "That is true," she said, then narrowed her eyes. "If I had to guess, I would say you were stalling to give yourselves more time."

"She's right," Ana finally spoke. "They'll show up."

Alexis didn't recognize her voice. The slight Russian accent was still there, but there was no hint of emotion. What'd happened to her? Maybe she wasn't as free as she seemed. Maybe it was all a game to unhinge them even more. The gun probably wasn't even loaded and this was all a setup. Ana couldn't be with the Reclaimers now. She'd rather die before joining a group like that.

Or would she?

The question surprised her, coming from somewhere deep within her. Of course, Ana would. She cared about others. It had to be something else.

"Well, we will wait then," Jezz said, turning and starting back toward the door. Ana followed her, avoiding any eye contact.

"Oh, where is my mind?" Jezz stopped and turned around. "We are not finished yet. I still have to honor my word—one of you must be reclaimed."

"I will," Alexis said immediately. "Reclaim me."

Jezz regarded her. Those blue eyes were too intelligent for someone who was clearly insane. Jezz's eyes searched hers as Alexis held the gaze of her killer. Even though she was determined to save the rest of them, she couldn't hold back the sudden fear as a feeling of intense regret at opening her mouth settled on her. What had she been thinking, offering herself to die? She almost took it back—almost.

"Do not rush it," Jezz finally said. "Now, which one of you wants to live?"

The question roused the last few people who'd been staring at the ground and they glanced up, looking toward Jezz. The woman smiled, showing her teeth. On anyone else, this would be a friendly gesture, but it made Jezz seem even more menacing than usual. The look in her eyes—the unadulterated gaze of someone who cared nothing for the lives of others—told Alexis that she had a goal in mind, whatever that was, and she would kill everyone to achieve that goal. Or maybe killing them all *was* her goal. She kept mentioning "reclaiming," and they were called Reclaimers. Perhaps that was just a fancy way to say murder.

"You have a choice," Jezz continued now that she had everyone's attention, "the same choice I gave my new acquaintance here." She motioned toward Ana, who was standing stone-faced next to her. "Kill and you can live."

"Oh, I'll kill you," Greg growled under his breath.

Jezz's gaze snapped to him. He held her eyes for six heartbeats, then looked down.

"One of your own," Jezz said, looking around the room at the gathered prisoners. "You will take the handgun, which has only one bullet, and shoot one of your friends in the head. A life for a life. Simple."

Alexis narrowed her eyes at Ana. She hadn't... had she? The guards had taken Ana and Mila from the barn. Now, Jezz was giving them the choice to kill one of their own to save their own life. Ana was here. Mila was not. Did that mean Ana had killed her? Who could enter into a bargain like that? It would be like trading one's soul to live for a few more days. But was killing to protect any different?

"I will," said Evan, the man with the tattered t-shirt who'd lost his family.

Evan? He didn't seem like that kind of man. Then again, he was full of pain, but Alexis still had a hard time believing he would kill one of his friends to save his own life. He'd lived in Burns for years and knew all these people, except her. Evan glanced over at her and then quickly away.

Oh, no.

"Marvelous," Jezz said.

She motioned forward a guard who'd appeared at her side, the same man who'd taken Ana and Mila. What was his name again? Max? He walked over to Evan and unchained him. Hauling Evan to his feet, Max prodded him forward, but Evan took one shaky step and fell to the ground.

"My legs are numb," Evan said.

"Give him a few minutes, Max," Jezz said. "Let the full implication sink in. I only want those who truly mean what they say, not weaklings afraid to die."

Max grunted in response.

Evan lay on his side, legs fully extended. His eyes were closed and he looked pained, but whether that was from the ache of regaining the feeling in his legs or the fact that he was about kill someone, she didn't know. She was no longer sure she wanted to die to save them if they were just going to kill each other off, one by one.

More than likely he'd choose her. She was the stranger here, the outcast in their little group. The rest of these people had years' worth of history together, and she only had a couple of days. He'd pick her; she would be the first to go. Surprisingly, she didn't resent that. The peace hadn't left her, even though she didn't know what to think or believe.

Alexis looked over at Ana, hoping she would at least glance at her, but she wouldn't. Alexis wondered what had happened to her and whether she'd really killed Mila. She thought she knew Ana but they'd only known each other for a week. Did she really *know* her? The fact was, she didn't. She didn't know anything about her past, besides the fact that her father was a mobster. Nothing except that one fact. Now that she thought about it, she realized for the first time that Ana had avoided talking about her past. In all their days together on the road, all their downtime, and all their talks, she didn't know anything more about Ana than what she'd learned that first night in Safe Haven.

That isn't the truth, Alexis thought, *I know who Ana is, just not who she* was.

Ana was a loyal friend, someone who was capable, determined, and strong. She was a survivor. And then the pieces clicked into place for Alexis. Ana would survive. No matter what she faced, she would do what needed to be done to live. She *would* survive.

"You killed her," Alexis stated more than asked, looking directly at Ana.

This time Ana did look at her. Her face may have been impassive, but her eyes were anything but. Alexis could almost *feel* the anger and the regret, but most of all, the determination. She was a survivor. If given a choice to sacrifice a life to save her own, she would do it. Anger rose inside Alexis. How could she kill Mila just to save her own skin? The mere thought turned her stomach. Alexis could never do that; there was no way. However, Ana could and here she was, alive, with her hands covered in the blood of the innocent.

"How could you?" Alexis asked, as she stared into those green eyes.

"I did what I did to survive," Ana said, some of the anger coming out in her voice. "Just like you will, if you're smart."

"I'll never kill an innocent person to save myself," Alexis spat, fury rising within her. A small part of her brain told her she was overreacting, but that just made her even angrier.

"Then you will die here," Jezz said.

Alexis flinched. Jezz was leaning down, her face a few inches from Alexis. While staring at Ana, she hadn't even seen the woman move. Jezz smiled, showing that menacing grin again and Alexis instinctually shied away, the hairs rising on her arms and neck. Her instincts told her this woman was deadly, more deadly than anyone else in the room. It was like being chained up with a lion prowling around her, licking its chops. Actually, that probably would have been less frightening. A lion could be predicted.

"It is time," Jezz said, straightening up. "Get up and kill or you will die."

"Wait," Evan said, looking up at her. "That wasn't the deal."

"That was always the 'deal.' Kill or you die."

Evan glanced at Alexis again, his eyes pleading. He'd changed his mind. In the heat of the moment, he'd wanted the chance to live, but now that he'd had time to think about it, he wasn't sure if he could do it. But he no longer had a choice. Alexis nodded to him.

"No," Evan said, "I can't."

Jezz pointed toward him and Ana tore her gaze away from Alexis. Ana hesitated and Jezz glared over at her.

"Are you with me or not?" Jezz asked in a low, threatening voice.

Ana fingered something at her neck, looking Jezz directly in the eyes. They stared at each other for a moment and then Ana moved. Walking over to Evan, she raised the handgun, pointing it directly at his head.

"The choice," Jezz said, "One last chance. Live or die."

Evan looked into the muzzle of the handgun and shivered.

"Okay!" he blurted out. "Okay, I'll do it."

He stood up with difficulty. Once he was on his feet, he glanced around the room. The looks people gave him ranged from fear to horror, anger to betrayal. He visibly withered under their gazes. He wasn't a murderer. Jezz walked over to him, handing him a long-bladed knife.

"Now, pick anyone you want," Jezz said, spreading her hands around the room, "and cut their throat."

"What?" Evan asked, blanching. "I thought... I thought you said I could just shoot them."

"I changed my mind. Prove to me that you have what I am looking for. If you cannot cut the throat of your friends, how can I trust you?" Jezz said, eyeing Evan like a bird of prey.

Evan was shaking now, the knife blade vibrating in his hand. Without looking at her, he walked toward Alexis with leaden steps. Could he really do it? If he killed her, he'd live, and her life would have meaning. She would have—unwillingly—given it to save someone. She didn't *want* to die, but she did want to make a difference.

Not in this way, she thought. *I want to save someone's life, not condemn them to the life of a murderer.*

She watched Evan as he drew closer, his steps taking longer and longer until, finally, he stood in front of her. The knife blade reflected the fading light from the open door, leading outside. The sun was setting. It'd been a whole day and yet neither her dad nor James and Connor had shown up. Were they all dead? Evan raised the knife, staring at the gleaming surface of the blade. It'd been honed to a razor-sharp edge and would cut through the soft flesh of a throat with ease. Alexis could almost feel the blade sliding across her throat. She shuddered. This was not what she wanted.

"I can't," Even croaked, dropping the blade to the dirt as a sob escaped his throat.

Alexis stared up into his eyes, showing her appreciation. She didn't want to die like this. A small smile spread on his lips as he looked down at her.

"Too bad," Jezz said, nodding.

Ana pulled the trigger and a deafening thunderclap filled the barn. The bullet smashed into the side of Evan's head, blowing a portion of his face off. Chunks of flesh, bone, and brains filled the air. Alexis had never seen anything so horrible in all her life. Blood splattered on her as Evan's body collapsed to the ground and she screamed. There was no other rational response to what she'd witnessed, and she knew she'd never get that image out of her mind. With speckles of blood on her face and the front of her shirt, she locked gazes with Ana.

"You're a monster," Alexis said, tears gathering in her eyes. "How did I ever consider you my sister? You've taken two innocent lives!"

Ana looked her square in the face, a wild look in her eyes. "I've killed more than that."

8

THE CUCKOO'S NEST

"Well, this blows," Tank said.

"Ya think?" Connor said. "This has been one goat-rope right after another since the very beginning."

"They've killed someone by now," James said in a hushed voice.

"We've got more pressing matters," Connor said.

"But—" James began.

"We're prisoners and probably gonna be dead soon," Connor said. "We can worry about the others if we survive."

"You're right," James said, closing his eyes and taking a deep breath. "We need to get out of here and then worry about the others."

Good, Connor thought, *he's still fighting.*

Connor looked around. They were all seated, handcuffed and chained to the brush guard on the front of the Hummer, arms level with their heads. James was towards the driver's side, Connor was next to him, and then Tank and Chloe were towards the passenger side. The man had held James hostage while Connor had been forced to handcuff Tank and Chloe. Next, Connor had cuffed himself, and then the guy had chained up James. He was now taking all their guns and gear from the back of the Hummer and setting them down on the ground a few yards away, all the while talking to himself. The only good news was that he'd spared them instead of killing them.

"None of ours... nope..." the man said as he stood over the pile of their gear.

"You lookin' for somethin'?" Tank asked.

The man's head snapped up. "What?"

"I said, are you looking for something?"

"Yes, missing gear, guns, people," the man said and he glanced to his right. "We've recovered most, but we're still missing some."

"That's all the gear we have," Connor said.

"We see that," the man said.

Tank looked at Connor, mouthing, "We?" Connor just shrugged. The man was probably crazy, which would fit with how everything else was going.

"What's your name?" Chloe asked, and the man looked over at her. "I'm Chloe."

"Bryce," the man said, turning and walking away from them.

"Where the hell are you goin'?" Tank asked.

"We need to think," Bryce said.

"Just let us go. We'll leave and never come back!" James shouted at him. "People are going to die if you keep us here."

"We don't care," Bryce said, walking into the last pavilion.

"Let us go!" James yelled as Bryce disappeared inside.

"What do we do now?" Chloe asked.

"Try and find a way to get loose," James said. "Any ideas?"

"Well, if we had a saw we could cut through the chains, or our hand if we had to," Tank said.

"Yeah, and how well did that work for Merle?" Chloe asked.

"*You* watched *The Walking Dead*?" Tank asked.

"Of course," Chloe said. "I thought it was an interesting concept... though I don't like it so much anymore."

Tanked laughed. "It's all a little too real now, isn't it?"

"Yeah," Chloe said, "just a little."

"C'mon, guys," James said. "We need to find a way out."

"James," Connor said, "you need to be prepared to face the reality that we might be here for a while."

"Then that leaves us with convincing Bryce to let us go," James said.

"You really think he's going to just do that?" Connor asked.

James shrugged. "Only one way to find out," he said, then shouted. "Hey, Bryce!"

After a few moments, Bryce poked his head out of the pavilion. "What do you want?"

"I have to pee," James said.

"Pee?" Bryce said. "We just chained you up."

"I know, but I had to go before—"

"We don't care," Bryce said, interrupting him.

"Then will you at least let me tell you why we're here?" James said, growing more desperate.

"Once again, we don't care. Just leave us alone so we can figure out what we're going to do with you," he said and went back into the pavilion, mumbling to himself.

"Pee?" Tank asked. "What are you? A twelve-year-old girl?"

"Shut up," James said, "I just wanted to see if it worked."

"Well, maybe if you'd talked like a man and said you had to piss, he might've let you go," Tank said.

"Will you just shut up and let me think?"

"Fine. When you come up with your master plan, let us know will ya, because I'll have to tinkle soon," Tank said.

Connor chuckled. "Leave him alone. We really *should* be trying to think of something."

"I know," Tank said. "I already went through all our options, and our best bet is to catch Bryce off guard and overpower him, maybe find a way to lure him over here and then somehow take him down."

"With all our hands chained?" Chloe asked.

"It still needs work, but that's the best option we have," Tank said.

"It could work," James said, "and once we get loose, there's a bunch of guns and other gear in that last pavilion."

"Really?" Tank asked.

"Yeah, over a dozen high-tech-looking combat rifles, plate carriers, helmets with NVGs, the works."

"Damn," Connor said. "Wish we could get that."

"Yeah," James said.

"How about we..." Chloe started but then trailed off.

"Yes?" Tank asked.

"I lost it," she said, "but it would've been a good one."

"I got it!" Tank exclaimed. "Chloe, you can take your shirt off and seduce him."

"You are such a—" Chloe said, kicking at Tank.

"Whoa, whoa!" Tank said, trying to get out of her reach. "I meant it as a compliment!"

Connor couldn't help himself; he laughed a little. The situation was just too comical. James joined in after a bit as Chloe continued to try to kick Tank, but her legs were just a little too short.

They were chained up and the Reclaimers had killed one of their friends, but they were chained up together and they were still alive. That was always a good thing, although if they could go just a few hours without something going wrong, it would be a new record. Connor was beginning to realize that wasn't possible anymore.

The sun beat down on them, burning their skin. It had to be over ninety degrees in the sun. James glanced up as beads of sweat rolled down his forehead and he licked his lips, tasting salt. It was the middle of the afternoon now. The Reclaimers would be killing someone else in a few hours. His mind flashed to an image of Alexis standing in all her tactical gear, ready to kick some zombie ass with her long brunette hair pulled into a ponytail, her hazel eyes sparkling in the light, and a smile tugging at the corners of her lips. His heart ached and he chided himself for those feelings. If she was executed, he'd never forgive himself. He renewed his efforts to think of a plan to escape. Over the course of the morning, they'd tried to get Bryce to come out of the pavilion with a myriad of prompts—pleading for help, to talk, to barter, threats—everything they could think of, but he hadn't so much as responded to any of them, so they'd given up on that.

Now, they sat, baking in the hot sun, wishing for just a hint of cloud cover to relieve them. James wished he'd put sunscreen on that morning. His face and arms would be burnt to a crisp by tonight, if they lived that long. His ear had begun to itch horribly, but he had to be careful with how sensitive it was. Also, his side ached and it felt like the blood had dried, sticking the bandage to the gash. Why did he always have to be the one who got shot? Connor had only been grazed and not even that bad. He wondered how they always seemed to find themselves in these kinds of situations, or better yet, how they were going to get out of this one. *Were* they even going to get out of this?

James cursed under his breath as the guilt and regret at helping the group leave Burns rose to the forefront of his mind, and he had to work hard not to let it overwhelm him. Whenever he thought about how he should've left them there, he thought of little Olive. She would never have left the school alive. More than likely, none of them would have. If that zombie horde had made it into the school, it would have been a mass slaughter, and he'd been able to help save some of them from that. But now, if he didn't make it to the Reclaimers' hideout, people would die as a direct result of his actions.

Help us, Lord, James prayed. *I'm at the end of my rope. We have people counting on us, and yet, we're stuck here. I surrender this to you. Take control. I trust you...*

The last few lines had been the hardest to say. Even though he was chained to the front of a Hummer with the hot summer sun beating down on him, having tried everything he could think of to escape, it was still extremely difficult for James to release control. This had to be his biggest flaw—the weakness that would get him killed. He felt like he needed to be in control, but he knew that thought was ridiculous. He *needed* to? He was just barely an adult in age and sure as hell not in attitude, yet he thought he knew better than everyone else around him. Well, not everyone, but most. Regardless, if he could handle a situation better, he still felt like he had to be in control.

It was the reason people hadn't liked him in school. He strove to be the best, but even when he wasn't, he'd give his input whether it was asked for or not. And he'd always felt the need to correct people when they were wrong, which had even caused him and Tank to get into a bunch of arguments. They'd spent almost one whole semester not talking because of a huge disagreement brought on by this very stubbornness. Well, that and there may have been a girl involved. The point was, he was nosey and needed to be in control.

He needed to be in control! The realization hit him as he sat there, and he wondered why he hadn't figured it out before. That was why he had such a hard time trusting that God knew the best plan for him. In a subconscious part of his mind, James always thought he knew better. He thought he knew better than God! He chuckled at that and his brother glanced over at him.

"What?" Connor asked.

"Nothing, just thinking," James said.

"You're not talkin' to yourself again, right?" Tank asked.

"I haven't done that in years," James said.

"Bro, I just heard you doing it last week," Connor said.

"What a weirdo," Tank said. "Who would talk to themselves like that?"

How could James, even subconsciously, think he knew better than God? The concept was just so wrong. Every time he tried to take control, it'd failed. Yet, when he surrendered and trusted God, things seemed to work out. It was time to stop trying to take control, stop pretending he knew better than God and everyone else. It was time for him to trust. In that moment, he fully surrendered the situation—being captured, the safety of the rest of their group, getting to Alaska, all of it. He gave it all to God. The peace that settled on his heart and soul was more refreshing than a cold drink of water, and he wondered why he'd been fighting so hard.

Thank you, Jesus, James said, smiling. *I know you've got my back. I may be seeing you soon, so make sure to save me a place at the table.*

He closed his eyes and laid his head back against the hot metal of the brush guard as the answers to life seemed to fall into place. The world was in order again, and yet nothing had changed but his perspective.

9

SKELETON IN THE CLOSET

Post-outbreak day 7, evening

Ana stood outside the barn with the captives inside. The captives? They were *her* group! She was already starting to think differently. Clamping down on those thoughts, she pushed everything from her mind. She didn't trust herself right now. If she started thinking too much, she would break down. Taking a moment, she put her thoughts back into their boxes.

"Well done in there," Jezz said, turning to look at Ana. "You will make a fine addition to the Reclaimers."

Jezz proffered her hand. Ana hesitated only a moment, then took it in a firm shake. Jezz smiled and Ana had a hard time not killing the woman right then and there.

"Since you will be joining us, I will show you to your room," Jezz said, turning to leave. "Max, put your best guards in place. I do not want our guests trying anything tonight."

"Yes, ma'am," Max said, moving to the two guards outside the barn door.

Jezz started walking down the dirt road leading to the rest of the compound and Ana followed. The temperature had dropped a few degrees as the sun sank behind the hills. It wouldn't set for another hour, but it was gone from the valley. The day had passed and she was still alive. She didn't know how she felt about that.

As they walked, Ana compiled a mental image of the compound. When she'd first seen it all this afternoon, she'd been impressed. They'd found the perfect place to set up their base. There were three different houses on the property, nine outbuildings, and six RVs, where most of the Reclaimers lived. She wasn't able to get a good estimate of how many Reclaimers there were, but she guessed over two dozen. She still wasn't sure where they were holding the kids; however, that didn't matter unless she decided to help them all. Her mind wasn't made up yet.

The compound sat at the head of a valley, surrounded by hills on three sides. The valley stretched north and the driveway followed it. She didn't know exactly where they were, but from what she'd gathered, they were east of the interstate somewhere.

The Reclaimers weren't what she'd expected. Not all of them were cold-blooded killers. Some just saw killing as something that needed to be done so they could continue to survive. Then there were the others like Jezz, who loved killing. They were the dangerous ones. She hadn't been able to move freely throughout the compound since Jezz made sure she was never far. The woman didn't trust Ana yet. She was clever.

They arrived at the house farthest from the pole barn. The six RVs were parked around the house and this was the most densely packed spot on the whole compound. That was no accident. There was a man with an AK-47 outside the door to the house. Jezz nodded to him and he opened the door. Inside was a quaint living room with a TV and two couches. The left part of the room was the kitchen and dining area. There was a small hallway leading to the right with three doors. A man was sitting on the couch with a Glock holstered on his hip. He stood up while quickly shoving a bottle of amber liquid behind his back. Jezz ignored him and walked down the hallway to stand outside the last door. As Ana walked by the man, she could smell the booze on him. If this man was her guard tonight, she should have little trouble getting out.

"This is your room now," Jezz said, as Ana walked up to her. "Someone will bring food shortly. You will stay here tonight under watch. Forgive me if I do not trust you yet."

Ana nodded. She'd expected as much. She offered Jezz the Glock she still held.

"You keep it," Jezz said, "as a reminder."

Ana didn't need the handgun to remember what she'd done that day. Walking into the room, she looked around. It was simply furnished, with a barred window set in the back wall, a queen bed on the left, and a dresser and small bathroom to the right.

"And Ana," Jezz said, "you will fit right in with us. You have that killer instinct. I can see it in your eyes."

Jezz smiled and shut the door, and Ana heard a lock clicking into place. She stood in the middle of the room, trying to force her thoughts into order but failing. Looking down at the Glock, she dropped it to the floor and sank to her knees as tears streaked down her face. She'd killed two people today, two *innocent* people. There was no coming back from that. It'd taken her years to forget about the last person she'd killed. Her mind shut down and she curled up on the floor.

She was a killer, always had been. No matter how fast or far she ran, she couldn't outdistance that single most damning fact of her existence. Most of her life had been dedicated to forgetting the past, and it was the only way she'd been able to survive this long. Now, in the course of a day, her self-control had almost completely eroded and the memories were close to bursting from their boxes.

No! she screamed in her mind.

Needing something to latch onto to make her forget, her hand reached for her locket and she began to rub it, taking comfort in old habits. She found her anger and unlocked the box it was contained in. Immediately, the tears stopped. So what if she'd killed two people? Because of that, she'd saved herself, and hopefully Alexis.

That bitch! Ana thought. *How dare she judge me?*

Didn't Alexis know what it'd cost to do what she'd done? Didn't she know that no matter what, Ana would never be the same after today? And she'd done it for Alexis, no less! She'd done it to rescue her! But Alexis dared to look at her like that, with all that judgment in her eyes? Ana almost wanted to leave and let Jezz kill them all. She could just disappear into the night. Or she could stay and truly join them. Some dark part of her wanted that. She could join them and let that side of her out into the open. No more hiding, no more trying to restrain it. Let it out and feel the power.

I can't!

She'd made a promise to Uncle Zeke a long time ago. Control. She had to remain in control. That other part of her would wreak havoc with who she truly was. It was the opposite of control and she *always* had to stay in control. Plus, she owed a debt, and debt had to be repaid, no matter the cost. Rescuing Alexis would pay that and then she could worry about the rest after. She just had to find a way to get out of the room and to the pole barn unseen.

Her mind began to run through a list of possibilities. A half hour passed and she'd moved to a more comfortable position on the bed. Her plan still needed a few tweaks, but it was coming together. She'd always been able to plan and strategize in a way that impressed her father. That was why he'd always come to her before making important decisions. She could see the complications and consequences of his actions, and she'd become her father's top advisor and at the age of just sixteen.

A knock sounded at the door.

"Come in," Ana said.

The empty Glock sat on the table by the door since there was no need to try to hide it. The same guard who'd been outside the house earlier brought her a tray of food. There was a plate of spaghetti, a salad, and a can of Dr. Pepper—a fine dinner for the apocalypse. He set the tray down on the table, eyeing the Glock but leaving it where it lay, and then left the room without saying a word. She noticed a slight wobble in his stride; the effects of the alcohol were setting in. He shut the door and she heard the lock click into place again. She walked over and took the tray of food to the bed.

As she ate, her mind mulled over the plan, trying to find the weak points. There was only so much more thinking and picking it apart she could do. Even with all the planning in the world, it came down to chance. That was the one thing she'd learned while working for her farther—either it worked or it didn't. This plan would only work if carried out soon, very soon. She would make her move tonight when everyone was asleep. When the morning came, she and Alexis would both be free of this place. Or dead.

10

BRYCE'S FRIEND

Post-outbreak day 7, early evening

T he afternoon passed and the sun neared the horizon. The Reclaimers would be killing the second survivor soon. James felt grief in his heart and a desire to help them, but it was tempered with the reality of their situation. They were chained up and weren't going anywhere. His epiphany earlier in the day had changed his perspective. It hadn't, however, magically freed them, like some would've expected. Intervention from on high was rare. More often than not, it was the internal changes that mattered the most. He was at peace, and maybe being at peace would affect those around him.

"You finally lose it?" Tank asked.

"What?" James asked, being pulled from his thoughts.

"Your mind. Did you finally lose it?" Tank asked again.

James chuckled. "Not yet, just surrendering control."

"Ah," Tank said. "You been prayin'?"

"Yeah."

"What'd ya hear back?" Tank asked.

"That everything will work out somehow."

Tank nodded. "I'm glad you're back to normal."

"Thanks," James said.

"He has to come out of there at some point, right?" Chloe asked. "I could use some water."

"I could go for that and some aloe," Connor said.

"Amen to that, brother," Tank said.

"Nah, just some water," Chloe said.

"That's because your tanned skin protects you from the worst of it," Tank said. "Although it does look like you got a little burned."

"Doesn't feel too bad," Chloe said.

"I'm pretty sure I look like a lobster," James said.

"You do," Tank said. "Trust me. I have intimate knowledge of lobsters."

"Wait, what?" Chloe asked. "Actually, never mind."

"Not like that!" Tank said. "I used to bartend at a seafood restaurant. Geez, get your mind outta the gutter."

"If it was anyone else, I wouldn't be worried. But you?"

"She does have a point," Connor said.

"Ha, ha," Tank said. "You guys are hilarious."

"So what do you think now?" James said. "Should we try and get him over here again?"

"Might as well," Connor said.

"Hey, Bryce!" Chloe yelled. "Could you bring us some water, please?"

A minute passed with no response, just the fluttering of the pavilions in the soft breeze. The wind felt good on James's skin. It was a welcome reprieve from the intense heat of the afternoon.

"Hey, Bryce!" James called louder. "We need some water!"

"Will you shut up!" Bryce yelled from inside the pavilion. "We're trying to think in here!"

"We'll keep yelling until we draw all the zombies for miles unless you bring us some damn water!" Connor yelled.

"C'mon, man!" Tank yelled.

"Please!" Chloe yelled.

"Fine!" Bryce yelled, storming out of the pavilion. He entered the middle one and came out with a case of water in his hands. Walking over to them, he threw the water down on the ground between them.

"Happy?" Bryce asked.

"Very. Thanks," Chloe said, smiling sweetly at him.

"Any chance you'd be willing to hear our side of the story?" James asked calmly.

Bryce looked at him. It seemed like he was about to respond but stopped, searching James's eyes.

"We thought you were the most unhinged before," Bryce said. "You look... different now."

"I feel much better," James said. "I just needed to have a little talk with myself."

"Yeah, we know what you mean," Bryce said. "We often have to give the other space. Otherwise, we'll drive each other crazy." He nodded to his right.

James looked but couldn't see anything he might've been referring to. "Umm... who're you talking about?"

"What do you mean?" Bryce asked, looking confused. "He's standing right there." He pointed to the spot next to him like there was someone in plain sight.

"Oh," James said.

"I see him," Tank said.

"Good. I didn't want to have to kill you," Bryce said. "The only people that can't see Elliot are crazy."

Tank choked on a laugh. Bryce narrowed his eyes at him, reaching for the handgun at his hip.

"Don't mind him," Chloe said. "All our throats are dry. We've been hacking all day."

Bryce moved his hand away. "Well, you have plenty of water now."

"Any chance we can get some food?" Chloe asked, batting her eyelashes.

Bryce looked at her, a smile tugging at his lips. "I think she likes you, Elliot," he said, nudging the air next to him.

Tank coughed again, hocking up some spittle and spitting it out on the ground. "Sorry, I should probably take a drink."

"Yeah," Bryce said. "I'll go get some food."

"And maybe a few blankets if we're going to spend the whole night out here," Chloe added.

"Sure," Bryce said, continuing to walk away. He disappeared into the middle pavilion again.

"Nice," Connor whispered.

"I told you layin' on the charm would work," Tank said. "Although it might just be that our captor likes crazy."

"What are you implying?" Chloe asked.

"Oh, nothing," Tank said. "Help me get this case of water."

They spent two minutes trying to move the case of water with nothing but their legs and feet. By the time Bryce returned, they'd only been able to move it a few inches. He tossed a handful of blankets and protein bars on the ground by the water and then turned to leave.

"Hey man, we might have a problem," James said.

Bryce turned back, finally noticing their failed attempt to get the water.

"If you could un-cuff one of our hands," Connor said, "we could just grab it."

"Okay," Bryce said and pulled keys out of a pocket, drawing his handgun, "we give Chloe the keys. She un-cuffs one hand and locks the empty cuff to the cattle guard. Then she'll have a free hand to get the stuff."

"It'd be easier if you just let us all have one hand free," Connor said.

"Do you think we're stupid?" Bryce asked, anger rising to his face.

"No," Connor said. "I just—"

"That sounds perfect," Chloe interrupted. "Thank you for your generosity."

"See, at least she has some manners. You'd make a great mother," Bryce said, eyeing her.

He brought her the keys, all the while keeping his handgun pointed at them. She unlocked her right hand and then cuffed the second loop to the brush guard, tossing the keys back. Bryce caught them without even looking. The whole time he had his eyes on the three of them. It would be hard to get the jump on him; however, that was still their best option. They just had to wait for the right opportunity. James had been ready to act, but Bryce was too far back and had never taken his eyes off of them.

"Now, we're going to go figure out what to do with you," Bryce said. "If you need anything else, too bad." He then looked at Chloe. "Unless *you* need something."

He smiled at Chloe and then walked off. Tank started laughing, but Chloe elbowed him in the side and he coughed instead. Bryce didn't look back as he entered the last pavilion, and Tank started chuckling.

"I think our friend here has an imaginary companion named Elliot," Tank said, between laughs.

"That's the name of the dragon in *Pete's Dragon*!" James said.

Everyone started cracking up.

"That's why you were bustin' a gut," Connor said when he'd caught his breath.

"I barely held myself together," Tank said. "I'm just glad he didn't start calling himself Pete."

After the laughter settled down, they were able to push the water and blankets close enough for Chloe to reach with her free hand. She tossed each of them a bottle of water, which they struggled to catch, and they chugged it down. After they'd eaten a protein bar, she gave them all a blanket, and they were barely able to drape it over themselves. The sun had set and it was cooling off quickly. It would probably drop into the fifties overnight. On its own, that wasn't cold, but the added wind-chill and fact they were seated on the ground would make it feel even colder.

"Well, I feel a lot more alive," James said. "There for a little bit, I thought I was going to turn into a zombie just from lack of water."

"At least we can spend the night in relative comfort," Tank said. "Although you know what this means."

"What?" Chloe asked.

"Now that we've had somethin' to drink, we'll have to piss soon," Tank said. "But I'm not goin' to ask Elliot if I can tinkle!"

"You still goin' on about that?" James asked. "I didn't say 'tinkle.' I said 'pee.' Plenty of adults say pee. Right, bro?"

"I'm not getting in the middle of this one," Connor said. "I'm already in between you two—literally."

"Just admit it, Jamesy Boy," Tank said. "You need to go tinkle."

"Whatever," James said with a laugh, shaking his head. "That little interaction with Bryce showed us some key things on how to take him down."

"First," Tank said, "he's batshit crazy and has an imaginary dragon named Elliot."

"We don't know yet if it's a dragon," James said, chuckling.

"True," Tank said. "His imaginary unknown entity."

"Second," Connor said, "he doesn't trust us."

"But Elliot trusts Chloe and Bryce likes her," Tank said with a wink. "I mean, did you hear that comment about her makin' a good mom? That's weird, even comin' from a crazy person."

"Why a wink?" Chloe asked.

"What wink?" Tank asked.

"That wink, just now," Chloe said.

Tank shrugged. "Sometimes I think I have Tourette's."

"You're ridiculous," Chloe said.

"No, he really does," James said.

"You know," Chloe said, "I've seen how you all act when you're apart and you actually seem your age. But when you get together, you act like three little boys in middle school."

They all looked at each other and shrugged.

"Yeah, pretty much," Tank said.

"Now, back to the plan," James said. "We find a reason to get him over here, then, Chloe, you lay some moves on him and we somehow take him down."

"'Somehow take him down?'" Tank asked. "I can feel the confidence in your plan oozing from just that comment."

"It needs a little work," James admitted. "I'm just not sure how to take him down."

"Yeah," Connor said. "We need to work on that."

They settled in, finding a halfway comfortable position. James hadn't realized it when he thought he was dying of thirst, but he was very uncomfortable. He never imagined he'd spend a night handcuffed to the front of a vehicle. He gazed at the sky, watching as the stars started to appear and the night deepened around them. Shifting, he was able to mostly wrap the blanket around himself, which helped cut the chill considerably. It would be a cold, uncomfortable night. Not the worst he'd ever had, but it would be close.

Closing his eyes, he began to remember the one night that had been much worse. He'd been guiding a client on a sheep hunt in Alaska and a black bear had come into camp when they were out hunting, demolishing their tents and eating their entire food supply. They'd had to spread the pieces of their tents over some branches and sleep underneath. Of course, as soon as they settled in, the rain had started to pour. James and his client had stayed mostly dry that night, fully bundled in all their clothes and raingear, but it'd still been a miserable night. Even before the apocalypse, he'd been in some hairy situations on hunting trips up in the mountains, but he'd survived all that and he'd survive this, too. Although this did take the cake for his most brutal survival experience yet. Trying to stay alive in the mountains was a lot easier than trying to stay alive with zombies and murderers at every turn.

His mind drifted to Alaska. How he missed those mountains. It would be the best day of his life when they finally reached the small bush airport where they could fly out to the lodge. It would take a few trips to get everyone into camp, depending on the size of the plane available. The lodge would have a lot of what they needed, but they'd initially spend a few days gathering as many supplies as they could. Then every week or so, they'd fly out and restock. They'd be able to have a life out there, away from all this. With the mountain ranges, rivers, bogs, and lakes to cross, there would be no way the zombies could get to them. The pucker brush alone would be enough to tangle their feet and trip them up. Very few people had ever hiked out to their lodge, and those who did were hardcore backpackers. The only reasonable way in was a bush plane or a two-day horseback ride.

Maybe they could find some horses and ride them out there. That would be a huge asset when it came to hunting and packing out their meat—especially moose since they weighed three-quarters of a ton. The gravel airstrip at the lodge was long enough that they could get a bigger plane in, if his brother could fly it. Maybe along the way, they could find another pilot. Then they could stockpile a bunch of planes out there and in the surrounding towns. Or maybe Connor could teach him how to fly, or even Tank. Tank would be good at flying—a little scary maybe, but good.

They could even build a wall and more cabins. There was a chainsaw mill already out there and they could bring more tools. There were endless possibilities. In the future, it could even become a settlement, a beacon of hope in the midst of the apocalypse. Last Hope—that's what they'd call it. If they did go that route, they'd have to set up a government, police force, schools, and all that. Finding enough people would take time, but it was doable. The hardest part would be the screening process so they didn't let psychos and murderers in. But at that point, they would have enough people for a police force and military. They would need strict laws—not oppressive laws but reasonable ones for the time. They could truly make a new life for themselves and others. It would be the start of something new, something beautiful. Life would continue, and humanity would survive.

Wrapped in the green wool blanket, James drifted off to sleep amid his pleasant dreams of what the future might hold.

11

JACKPOT

J ames woke up to screaming.
Not again!

He tried to grab his gun. Except he didn't have a gun, didn't even have a knife, and he was handcuffed to the front of a Hummer. Night had fully settled over the land, and he could just make out the others' silhouettes in the dim light of the half moon. The scream sounded again right next to him. It was high-pitched and feminine.

"Chloe, what's wrong?" Tank asked, sounding frantic.

"Help!" Chloe screamed. "Help me!"

James must've been in a deep sleep because he was finding it hard to gather his thoughts. If a zombie had ahold of Chloe, they were going to be next and they had no way of defending themselves. They would be dead. Bryce ran out of the pavilion, combat rifle aimed ahead and tactical light slicing through the darkness. James still didn't know what kind of rifle he had. It looked similar to an M16, but more sleek and sexy.

Why am I thinking about the rifle right now?

"Chloe!" Tank said, sounding concerned.

The emotion surprised James. When was the last time he'd truly seen Tank concerned? It wasn't that he never felt concern or fear—or anything—he just never *showed* it. But he was showing it now and

James was shocked. It was actually the most shocking part of the whole scene. Tank, concerned?

The light from Bryce's rifle landed on them, illuminating the scene. Chloe was doing her best to back away from the darkness on the other side of the Hummer. She was breathing heavily and whimpering occasionally, her eyes wide.

"Chloe," James said. "What's going on?"

"What the hell is it?" Tank asked.

Bryce arrived, looking them over before his gaze settled on Chloe. Concern flashed in his eyes.

"What happened?" Bryce asked Chloe.

Chloe tried to speak but couldn't get any words out. She was shaking now and beginning to cry. She tried to speak again, but ended up choking out a sob.

"Dude," Tank said. "What the hell?"

"What happened?" Bryce asked again, addressing them.

"I have no idea," James said. "I was asleep when she started screaming."

Connor stared at her, a confused and calculating look on his face. "Maybe she thought she saw something in the darkness."

"She's been through a lot," Tank said, "but I've never seen her like this."

She glanced up at Bryce, tears in her eyes. They left streaks on her face and she seemed completely unhinged. Bryce walked around them and went over to kneel down by her. He raised his hand, acting like he wanted to wipe her tears away. Stopping himself, he looked to his right.

"Elliot says we should take you back to our room," Bryce said. "It's safe there."

Chloe nodded sheepishly, like a little girl who'd had a nightmare and ran into her parents' bedroom. Bryce smiled, getting out the keys and taking her handcuffs off. When she was free, she embraced him in a tight hug. He looked momentarily taken aback, glancing over to his right again. Then he nodded.

"You'll be safe with us," Bryce said as Chloe separated from him.

She smiled tentatively as Bryce turned and led her to his pavilion. The whole way there he scanned the darkness, looking for any sign of a threat while Chloe stayed right behind him with her hand on his shoulder. They disappeared into the white flaps of the tent and light emanated from inside.

"What the hell just happened?" Tank asked.

"I have no idea," James said.

"A wolf in sheep's clothing," Connor whispered.

"What?" James asked.

"The Trojan horse," Connor said.

"Ya think?" Tank asked.

"That was a pretty convincing act if that's what she was doing," James said.

"Yeah," Tank said. "It scared the shit outta me."

"I'm telling you," Connor said, "she was faking it."

"I don't know," James said. "If so, what's she gonna do now?"

"What's necessary, hopefully," Connor said.

"Has she killed anyone that you know of?" James asked Tank.

"No, I haven't even seen her kill an undead yet," Tank said. "In fact, I'd put money down she hasn't."

"She did act surprisingly calm when helping Mike," James said. "But I don't know if she has it in her."

"We'll find out," Connor said.

"If she isn't faking, we'd better be ready to try something," James said. "I don't want to be chained up like some free Happy Meal for one of these zombies."

"Me neither," Tank said. "I hate being a sittin' chicken."

"I get the chicken part now," James said. "Our hands are cuffed and chickens can't fly."

"I knew you'd come around," Tank said.

The light in the tent went out, plunging their world into darkness again. James's mind began to play tricks on him and he could see moving shapes in the darkness around them. Closing his eyes, he took a few deep breaths, banishing the thoughts.

Had Chloe really been putting on an act? How could a person stage-cry like that? The fear in her eyes had looked real. Maybe she was a good actress. Even if she was, what would she do now? Kill Bryce? Handcuff him? There was no way she was going to overpower him. She was half his size. He continued trying to piece together whether it was possible, but he knew he was doing it to avoid the other questions his mind wanted to ask: If she hadn't been faking, what had she seen to make her freak out like that? What was out there with them?

"Guys," James finally said after a few minutes, "I don't think I can sleep now. I'm too... wired."

"Me too," Tank said.

"You guys are just—"

A gunshot cut off what Connor had been about to say.

James snapped his head to look over at the pavilion Bryce and Chloe had disappeared into. Another gunshot sounded, and this time James could see the muzzle flash from inside.

"Oh, shit!" Tank said.

"Did he just..." James began to ask but trailed off.

Chloe came running out of the tent, flashlight in one hand, handgun in the other. When she got to them, she dropped to her knees by Connor, the closest one to her. She set the handgun down and reached into her pocket, pulling out the handcuff keys. After he was free, Connor immediately picked up the handgun and aimed it in the direction of the pavilion as she moved to James and un-cuffed him, then Tank. She didn't start shaking until they were all free, and the tears began shortly after. Tank hesitated only a second and then stepped up, pulling her into his arms. She dissolved into tears.

"I didn't want... but he... I've never..." she choked out between sobs.

"Shhh," Tank said, stroking her hair. "It's okay. You did what you had to."

James went a few yards and grabbed his AR from the pile of their gear Bryce had left. Odd, he'd never even seemed interested in it once he'd learned it wasn't "his." James checked the magazine. It was full and he racked a round into the chamber. Aiming his AR at the far pavilion, he switched his tactical light on. He didn't know if Chloe had finished Bryce off or not, but he wasn't about to take any chances. Still aiming forward, he reached down and picked up his brother's AR, then stood up and brought it to him.

"Tank," Connor said, offering Tank the handgun, "get her into the Hummer and wait for our signal, then pull over to the pavilion."

"Got it," Tank said, leading Chloe around to the passenger's seat.

James grabbed their tactical vests from the ground and they slipped them on, all the contents still intact. He picked up the rest of their gear from the ground and tossed it into the back seat.

"Let's go," James said, as Connor took point.

Twin beams of light swept through the darkness in rotating intervals as they approached the pavilion. James went around to the entrance while Connor went to the hole cut in the side. They burst into the tent, lights sweeping the interior. The main room was clear. The curtain that sectioned off the small room was ripped open and inside laid Bryce, blood dripping through the cot and pooling on the ground. He'd been shot in the chest and head. She'd taken him out effectively. James noticed his right hand was hanging off the cot and below it was a handgun.

"He was armed," James said.

"She had no choice," Connor said. "She made the right call."

"I'm impressed," James said, looking around the room for any more threats.

"I told you," Connor said, "she's tougher than she lets on. Just like Tank, actually."

"They are very similar."

"It's probably why they argue so much."

"Wait, do you think—"

"Maybe, but that's a discussion for another time."

"True, let's collect what we need and go rescue our friends."

James moved farther into the pavilion, his gaze sweeping over all the gear and guns lying out on the cots. Almost every cot held a uniform, rifle, handgun, tactical plate carrier, helmet, and a few personal effects. Only six cots were missing items. The one closest to Bryce's room was missing a handgun. Maybe this was what Bryce had meant about finding his stuff. James checked and rechecked the room. When he was sure it was clear, he lowered his AR. Something felt wet on his side and he looked down, seeing that his wounded had opened again. He cursed.

"I'll signal Tank," James said.

"I'll start gathering all the gear," Connor said. "This is a jackpot!"

James exited the pavilion and flashed his light toward the Hummer. It roared to life, headlights coming on, and Tank pulled up next to the pavilion.

"What's the plan?" he asked, rolling down the passenger window.

"Gather all we can here and then make a game plan," James said. "If you want, there are some Kryptek uniforms in here. A bunch are unused. Plus a boatload of guns."

"Okay, I'll be in," Tank said, glancing at Chloe in the passenger's seat.

"Thank you," James said, looking at Chloe. "You saved us and the rest of my group."

Chloe nodded. "You're welcome."

"I'll have to ask you later how you got so good at acting," James said. "You had me fooled good."

A small smile grew on her lips. James turned and went back into the pavilion.

"Bro!" Connor exclaimed. "These are Bushmaster ACRs!" He held up the rifle Bryce had been carrying earlier.

"Really? I've never seen one in person," James said, coming over to where his brother was making a pile of them on one of the cots.

He picked one up. It felt like a dream come true with the smooth edges and sleek black exterior. It had a similar setup to an AR-15, which made him feel right at home. It was the weapon of a real man—or woman. The only downside was that it was a pound or so heavier than his AR, but other than that, it was impressive.

"This is awesome!" James said. "Don't these have the interchangeable barrels and the piston-operated action?"

"Yep," Connor said, "and they shoot 5.56 just like our ARs."

"Damn," James said, examining the ACR in his hands.

Most of them seemed to be fully loaded, with an angled foregrip, tactical light, IR laser, suppressor, and Trijicon 4x32 ACOG scope with a red dot on top—the perfect combination for both close quarters and long-range combat. Five of them were classified as DMRs and had longer barrels with a bipod and Vortex Razor 6-24x50 scope. Those were configured to be used at longer ranges.

Connor came from the sectioned off part of the room, holding a very large machine gun. Tank walked into the pavilion just then and noticed the gun Connor held. His mouth dropped open.

"Is that..." Tank started.

"A SAW," Connor finished. "I think it'll fit your tastes."

"Oh, hell yeah!" Tank said, and went over to take the large gun from Connor. "Oh, baby!"

The M249 Squad Automatic Weapon, or SAW, had a bipod, IR laser, suppressor, and Trijicon 4x32 ACOG scope. Tank lifted the gun into the air, smiling.

"It's lighter than I thought it'd be," Tank said.

"That's because it looks like it's the new lightweight variant," Connor said. "It's probably only fifteen pounds. But wait till you have the full two-hundred-round drum magazine. Then it'll push twenty!"

"I don't care," Tank said. "This thing is a beast!"

"And look at these," James said, showing Tank the ACRs.

"Damn, those are sexy," Tank said.

"Right?" James said.

"Enough ogling," Connor said. "Let's get our gear together."

They spent a few minutes setting aside what they were going to use. James organized all the extra gear into black canvas bags so every bag would have a little of everything. Tank and Connor then loaded the bags into the back of the Hummer. After that, they put some extra supplies—mainly ammunition—in four backpacks they'd found. That left them with ten fully loaded bags and one partial. Grabbing some of the boxes of MREs, protein bars, and water from the middle pavilion, they filled the back of the Hummer. Once done, they went back inside the last pavilion to change.

There was a first aid kit inside and Connor quickly redressed James's side and ear while Tank put on one of the unused Kryptek Typhon uniforms. Connor's shoulder had barely bled since the last time they'd bandaged it so James just put a Band-Aid on it. Having done that, they changed into matching uniforms, respectfully removing the nametags. The brothers outfitted themselves with plate carriers, complete with body armor and loaded with suppressed Berretta M9 handguns, six ACR magazines, four handgun magazines, a flashbang and boot knife. They then slipped on helmets with headsets and NVGs. Both of them held their newly acquired ACRs. Tank was similarly outfitted, minus all the 5.56 ammunition on his plate carrier. Instead, he had a fragmentation grenade and two flashbangs. He'd be carrying his extra two-hundred-round drum magazines for the SAW in his backpack.

"I feel like we might actually stand a chance now," James said.

"Wolf Pack!" Connor said, "What is your profession?"

"HA-OOH! HA-OOH! HA-OOH!" James and Tank yelled at the same time, lifting their guns into the air.

"Perfect," Connor said. "Get acquainted with your new toys. Then, we roll out."

"What the hell was that?" Chloe asked from outside in the Hummer.

"Just a little motivational speech," Tank said.

"It just sounded like yelling," Chloe said.

"Exactly," James said.

"You three are incorrigible," Chloe said.

"So, what's the plan?" Tank asked as he checked his SAW.

"I found their base, more than likely," Connor said.

"Okay," James said. "Chloe will stay up here with the Hummer and we'll go down into the hideout, find where they're keeping our group, and extract them."

"That should be our first priority," Connor said. "Then we can worry about killing the Reclaimers. Even though these things are suppressed, they'll still be loud enough for anyone awake to hear."

"Exactly," James said. "We'll need to be quick and quiet."

"Time to go kick some Reclaimer ass!" Tank said.

12

THE WOLFE

E mmett Wolfe lay on a ridge east of Sheridan, Wyoming, looking down on a large group of ranch buildings spread out in the bottom of a valley six hundred yards away, although now it resembled more of a compound than a ranch. The driveway came down from the red gravel road a mile away to the northwest. The driveway snaked past a collection of six buildings to the south, with a single large house to the north, and then continued up a little hill to the east where it ended in a "T." North of the "T" was a house and detached garage, south were three outbuildings—a large pole barn, covered carport, and a stable with a pen. The six buildings south of the driveway consisted of a small house, garage, two small barns, stable, and small shed. Between the stable and one of the barns was a large, fenced-in pen. In a semi-circle next to the small house was a group of six RVs. This seemed to be where most of the Reclaimers lived.

The large house north of the main collection of buildings seemed to be reserved for the higher-ranked members. Only six Reclaimers had entered there, along with the leader. Farther east and up the driveway where the other buildings sat was the large pole barn where his daughter and the rest of the captives were being held. North of that sat a detached garage where they were keeping the children.

The sun was sinking in the sky behind him, which gave him the perfect angle so his shadow would prevent the optics from glinting in the light. There were thirty-seven people living and working on this compound. Fifteen of those were always out—ten at the ambush spot and five scouts in the surrounding hills. They'd only left one blind spot and that was where he lay. It'd taken him most of the morning to climb up to this vantage point and look down on the inner workings of the Reclaimers. They held tight security, just not tight enough. The bush he was hidden in was big enough to conceal a person. They were smart, but they weren't professionals. They weren't trained to hunt people—to find weaknesses and exploit them.

Emmett was.

Case in point was how they'd botched taking him captive the evening before. Any professional could have seen what needed to be done and how to avoid it. Their technique would work on ninety-five percent of the population, but not him. All he'd had to do was offer his wrists in a way that he would be able to slip out of the zip ties. The man doing it had obliged by looping the zip tie around his wrist and tightening it as much as he could. Then he'd move on to the next one in line, never noticing that Emmett had his fists clenched tightly. That was the problem with having to restrain fourteen adults before they tried something. The Reclaimers had rushed and done a sloppy job. It'd been their undoing.

He pulled up the binoculars he'd taken and gazed down at the valley—studying his prey. These people, the Reclaimers, were an eclectic group of murderers. Some seemed more afraid of their own people than what was around them. The others went around bullying that group, their bloodlust insatiable. Then, there was the woman in charge. She hadn't been at the ambush on the interstate but Emmett still knew who she was.

This woman carried herself with an air of authority and had an aura of danger to her. The power she had over other people and the fear she caused them was a drug to her. He'd seen it overseas with the leaders of the Taliban and Al Qaeda. Seeing her more throughout the afternoon had just confirmed what he'd first thought. She was a tyrant, lording over her people with fear. He'd thought about sneaking in and ending her life, but that wouldn't solve the problem of his daughter being a hostage to a group of murderers. Getting her out was his first and main objective. Rescuing everyone else was secondary.

The events of yesterday played over in his mind and he wondered once again if he'd made the right call—not that there had been much of a choice with almost three dozen armed hostiles pointing at least six RPGs at their vehicles. There hadn't been many options. On the other hand, if he hadn't escaped, maybe he could've rescued his daughter more readily. That was a horrible notion, however, since he'd then be in the same place as her. At least now he could sneak in and rescue her. There'd been a few moments throughout the day when he'd almost gone in, but every time he'd waited, and it'd proven to be the right choice. There were just too many people down there, walking around. Without the cover of darkness, it would be almost impossible to infiltrate and execute a successful extraction. So he waited, impatiently, for the right moment.

Late in the evening, he caught a glimpse of something red out of the corner of his binoculars. A young woman with bright red hair was walking with the leader. Watching the way she walked and held herself, he wasn't surprised when he caught a glimpse of her face. It was Ana. She was free and walking alongside the leader with a handgun. What was going on down there? They both walked up to the pole barn where the captives were held. The guards opened the door for them and Ana strode in with the leader at her heels. The door shut. He watched the building for a few minutes, trying to judge what was going on. Had Ana betrayed them and joined the Reclaimers? No, that wouldn't happen.

Something popped down in the valley. He was over six hundred yards away, but the sound was unmistakable—a gunshot, small arms, probably a pistol. A little while later, the leader and Ana walked out of the barn. They paused outside the door and then continued down into the main collection of buildings. They entered the small house there, and a minute later the leader emerged without Ana. Was she being held captive there? Or maybe was she staying there of her own free will. Emmett couldn't be sure it was Ana who'd fired the shot, but she was the one who'd walked in and out with the gun. He hadn't noticed anyone else down there shooting at the time. What did that leave as possibilities? Either Ana had betrayed them or was playing along. He wouldn't assume anything until he could talk to her. Then he would work with that information.

For the hundredth time that day, he thought of what could be happening to his daughter. He wanted to rush in and free her, but it wouldn't do her a bit of good if he got himself killed. For all he knew, James and Connor were dead and he was his daughter's only hope. So he waited and prayed she was safe. To distract himself and maybe understand more about his enemy, he worked through their capture yesterday.

After the initial ambush, they'd separated the adults from the kids. Then a man named Max had given a speech about how they'd trespassed and would need to pay the price in blood. When his speech concluded, he'd grabbed Hank and gone back into the bus. That was when the big man had come over and restrained them, then loaded them up into vehicles. The Reclaimers hadn't planned for so many and they'd had to load Emmett into the last truck with three Reclaimers and no other prisoners.

Slipping his restraints had been quick and simple. The man next to him went down first with his own knife to his throat. Then, when the man in the passenger's seat had tried to aim his handgun at him, Emmett had grabbed his hand, redirecting it at the driver. When the Reclaimer fired, the driver had been hit. The truck swerved and Emmett gained the handgun. Switching his grip on it, he shot the man in the passenger seat, then finished off the driver.

The truck had crashed into a ditch. They hadn't been driving fast and he'd recovered quickly, getting out of the truck and grabbing a black bag from the bed. On his way out, he grabbed the passenger's rifle and took off into the creek bottom, east of the road. The driver of the vehicle in front of them hadn't been paying attention because he never turned around. Emmett had taken the time to get away from the scene while following the road from cover beside it.

After half an hour, the Reclaimers had returned to check on the missing vehicle. On their way back to their base, he'd tried following them but had lost them shortly after. It'd taken him all night to find where they'd gone. He'd checked over three dozen houses and a few different back roads along the way before he'd stumbled onto this place.

Now, he was lying on the ridge, waiting for night to fall. All the guns and gear he had were still in the black bag hidden under a bush down the ridge behind him—all but a Bushmaster ACR combat rifle. He'd chosen that as his main weapon for the assault and it lay next to him now. It was decked out with an angled foregrip, tactical light, IR laser, suppressor, and Trijicon 4x32 ACOG scope with a red dot on top. Where these people had gotten a weapon like that, he couldn't imagine. He'd thought maybe it was just a tasteful individual who'd had it. But when he'd opened the black bag, he'd realized that assumption was wrong. This bag held another Bushmaster ACR DMR, a black plate carrier, a couple of Beretta 9mm handguns, magazines for all of them, and a tactical helmet with NVGs and headset attached.

The gear was beyond anything these simple civilians should have, especially around Sheridan, Wyoming, of all places. There had to be a military or government outpost around here somewhere, or they had raided one somewhere. Emmett was glad for it. Even though it meant the Reclaimers were well armed, so was he. He itched to put the gear to use. All those people needed one thing—a bullet to the head—and he was going to give it to them. Unconsciously, he almost stood up to go down, but stopped himself.

Easy now, Emmett told himself, *you'll get your chance. You've waited way too long to rush in with only a few hours left to wait. Patience.*

The sun had set behind the Bighorn Mountains in the distance and darkness was beginning to creep in. Only a little while longer. Then, he would sweep into the compound like one of the ten plagues and rescue his daughter, killing anyone who got in his way. His years of training were the only thing holding him together now. Inside, the father in him was screaming to go down there and save his little girl, but he tempered the desire. He would get his chance, and when he did, neither heaven nor hell would stand in his way.

13

THE BEST LAID PLANS

Post-outbreak day 8, early morning

Tank followed behind James and Connor, breathing heavily. It wasn't that he was out of shape—well, actually he was. But it was also because those two skinny bastards in front of him had been doing this their whole lives. They would hike the mountains and hills with a bunch of gear on their backs almost every day in the fall, for crying out loud. Not him. Oh no, he spent most of his time at his desk or at work. He did go for a walk most days, but a walk in the city couldn't compare to practically running around the hills with fifty pounds of gear. It wasn't that he was struggling physically, much. They were just moving a little too fast and his asthma was on the fritz. Plus, he did happen to be carrying an almost twenty-pound gun with at least fifteen pounds in his backpack, not to mention the helmet and twenty-pound plate carrier.

After a mile of walking quickly, he was struggling, but he didn't let it slow him. He just kept going right behind them. He even kept pace with them when they seemed to move *faster* up the hillside. Near the top, the brothers dropped to the ground, crawling the rest of the way to the ridgeline. It didn't matter that it was night and no one would be able to see them without optical aid like the night vision they were wearing right now. The Andderson brothers didn't take chances. They played it as safe as possible, yet weren't afraid to act. It was why Tank felt safe, knowing they had his back, and they felt safe knowing he had their backs. Not once had they looked back to make sure everything was good. After all these years of being friends, they trusted him with their lives, even though they'd never before been in a situation where their lives were *actually* on the line.

They were his best friends in the world, brothers-from-another-mother, but they weren't blood. Growing up, he hadn't had anyone who had his back at home. It had just been him. When his mom remarried after the divorce, he'd acquired a step-brother who was older than Tank, and they'd never been close. James and Connor had always been more of his brothers than anyone else. Hell, they felt more like family than a lot of his extended family did.

That thought surprised him and he felt a familiar discomfort rising up. He sometimes felt that he was intruding by being friends with them. There was a bond between the two of them that nothing could break, and they had invited him into that bond. It was like he was their *actual* brother and they always treated him as such. But that didn't stop him from feeling like he was the third wheel at times. Not now, though. He wasn't worried about all that crap. It was time to act—time to make some heads pop.

Tank took a knee on the back side of the ridge below the brothers and looked behind him, checking their six. The darkness was illuminated in green. He'd never tried night vision in real life, only in video games. It was way kickass! The thing he hadn't expected was the lack of depth perception. Determining the distance of things was extremely difficult, and it took him awhile to get used to it. He'd almost stumbled a few times in the first few hundred yards or so, but he had the hang of it now. The coast was clear behind them—no Reclaimers and no undead.

He felt a little bad for Chloe, having left her all alone on the hilltop. She had one of the ACRs and a handgun, so she should be safe. But thinking about her brought their hug to the forefront of his mind, and he smiled. He'd acted on a whim, trusting his feelings. He was a bit confused though. He'd thought he hated her, so when had he begun to grow fond of her? No matter. He'd think about that later, but right now he had to focus on the task at hand. They had some people to rescue and some payback to hand out at the end of a barrel.

"What do you think?" James asked.

"There are a lot of buildings down there," Connor said.

"Looks like some sort of ranch," James said.

Tank crouch-walked up to them, sticking to the cover of a conveniently placed bush.

"I bet they're in one of those," Tank said, pointing at a collection of three outbuildings east of the main collection of buildings.

"What makes you think that?" James asked.

"Look at all those buildings," Tank said, pointing at a group of six closely placed buildings. "See all the RVs parked around them? That makes me think those are the living quarters, but those buildings over there are off by themselves, in the open."

"The logic is sound," Connor said.

"Your guess is as good as any," James said. "We can start at those, then move north to that lone house and then head down to the rest."

"We should stick to this side of the ridge and then loop around to the outbuildings instead of cutting it too close to the main ones," Connor said.

"What're we doing still sittin' here?" Tank asked. "Let's get the move on!"

"We thought you might want a break," James said.

"Oh, screw off," Tank said. "I'm doing a damn good job keepin' up."

"Actually, you are," Connor said, "and you have the twenty-pound gun!"

James chuckled. "I know you are, bro, but I had to get you back for all the 'Jamesy Boy' comments."

"Well, I hope you feel good about yourself for makin' fun of the fat kid," Tank said.

"You keep up the way you've been doing and you won't be able to say that for much longer," James said.

"True," Tank said. "I better find some pizza and a couple donuts tonight and fix that."

Laughing, Connor took the lead, with James following and Tank bringing up their six.

"So, Allen," James said, "are you always goin' by Tank now? Even when it's just us?"

"Yeah," Tank said. "I had a moment that first day of the apocalypse when I decided it would be a new start. I *am* Tank now."

"Fair enough," James said. "Wanted to ask when Chloe wasn't around."

"Yeah," Tank said. "Don't tell her."

"I may..."

"Shut up and keep walkin'," Tank said.

James laughed and continued to follow Connor. Staying on the back side of the ridge, they followed it south of the hideout. The hill sloped off and they descended into the bottom of a small cut. Following the cut led them right into the hideout from the southeast. They could see the group of three outbuildings with the pole barn, where the hostages hopefully were.

A shot sounded in the night, followed by two more. They stopped in their tracks, looking west where the main part of the hideout was. A few seconds later the gunfire picked up again and soon became a full-blown war zone. They could hear vehicles revving up. Tank looked at Connor, who was looking back at him and James.

"Check the pole barn," James said. "Then go investigate that. They may be fighting off another group."

Connor moved off, jogging toward the pole barn.

Tank and James followed. When they arrived at the barn, they noticed two dead guards lying outside. Connor stacked up at the side of the door as James and Tank joined him. Connor nodded and the brothers rushed into the building. Tank looked around one last time, then joined them inside, SAW shouldered and ready to kill.

The barn was empty.

14

RESCUE

Post-outbreak day 8, early morning

A na stood next to her door with the metal fork from dinner gripped in her hand while her mind worked through the possibilities of the plan once again. Everything hinged on this first part—getting out of the room. She just hoped it was the drunkard from before who'd be responding. She glanced at the handgun sitting on the table without a magazine in it. It would be useless now.

"Excuse me," Ana said, speaking towards the door. "I really need some water."

She waited, hoping it would be enough to draw the guard. A few minutes passed and she didn't hear anything from outside.

"Excuse me," Ana said a little louder this time.

This time she heard footsteps coming down the hall to her room.

"What ish it?" a male voice asked, slurring his words. It was the drunk. Perfect.

"Could I bother you for some water?" Ana asked.

"Why not use the sink in there?" the voice asked, speaking slowly.

"It's broken. Nothing comes out."

"Not again. Okay, let me get some."

Footsteps retreated from her door and she could hear him shuffling around in the living room. As he started to come back, she took a deep breath and the realization hit her with full force. This was it—her one chance to get out of here before morning. If she'd miscalculated or there was more than one guard, she would be dead.

"Get away from the door," the voice said.

"I am," she said softly with her head turned toward the inside of the room.

She heard the lock disengage and readied herself, raising the fork. The door opened and the man took one step into the room, water bottle in one hand, handgun in the other. Ana grabbed his closest arm, the one with the handgun, and slammed the fork into the man's throat with all her strength. The tines tore through the soft skin and entered his carotid artery. The man dropped the water bottle and raised his hand to his gushing throat while trying to bring his gun to bear on her. She locked her elbow and held his gun arm down while quickly jerking out the fork, accompanied by a spray of blood. She stabbed it in again, and the man choked and released the gun. Grabbing at her hand, he tried to remove the fork, but as his hand started to clamp down around her wrist, she brought her knee to his groin. Legs buckling, he fell to the floor, releasing her hand. Jerking the fork out again, she quickly stabbed it hard into his eye. Due to the loss of blood and disoriented from the pain, the man raised little defense as the fork popped his eye and entered his brain.

As the man fell to the ground, his blood quickly pooling on the carpet and a fork sticking out of his eye, Ana stood there, breathing heavily. Her face, chest, and right arm were covered in blood. A small part of her gazed at the crimson liquid pooling on the floor and smiled, but she quickly shoved that elation down, adopting a cold, emotionless state. Stooping, she picked up his handgun, a Glock 17 like the one sitting on the table in her room. She then searched his body, coming up with a holster for the Glock, a hunting knife, and two magazines. Going to the table, she loaded one of the magazines into her gun and stuck the man's gun into the holster, which she then strung on her belt. She tucked her own Glock into her pants at her back and the extra magazine in her back left pocket.

Grabbing the body of the man, she pulled him into the room and shut the door behind her, then moved through the hall with the large hunting knife held ready. In the living room, a man was asleep on the couch, AK-47 resting on the floor next to him. Stalking over, she stood above him, watching the rise and fall of his chest. This was the deciding moment. Did she kill everyone she could, or get out with as little killing as possible? She didn't care about the loss of life. These people were evil and deserved death. But the more she killed, the more she lost herself.

The choice was made for her as the man rolled over, stretching. She didn't wait to see if he was awake or just moving in his sleep. The knife drew a crimson line across his throat and his eyes popped open. He gasped for breath but couldn't catch one with a severed windpipe. In a matter of seconds, he was dead. She picked up the AK-47 and the two extra magazines from the coffee table. Slinging the rifle over her back, she shoved the two magazines into her pockets.

The outside door opened and a woman began to walk into the room. Ana moved with the speed and grace of a predator. The woman had barely cleared the door when Ana was on her, slashing the knife across her throat. The woman's eyes bulged and she dropped the shotgun she was holding. Ana stood as the woman collapsed to her knees.

Yes, that's right where you belong—at my feet, said a voice in her head.

Ana was shocked motionless. She hadn't heard that voice in years. It was both her and not her, a part she kept hidden. Closing down her mind, she moved all her thoughts into their boxes.

Ana hauled the body of the woman inside the house and then went outside, shutting the door behind her. The cool night air felt good as she breathed it in. She moved quickly, leaving the glow of the porch light and entering the shadows to the side of the building. It was around three in the morning and everyone but the guards should be sleeping. But now that there were three bodies, this would have to be quick.

Moving around the buildings, she stayed out of the light and headed toward the pole barn on the hill. Alexis would be sleeping in there. Ana's earlier anger at her had abated when she'd realized she was really angry with herself. How could she blame Alexis for judging her? For all Alexis knew, she'd done this just to save herself. That had been a part of it, but not the main part. Right?

She ascended the hill. There would be two guards posted by the pole barn and another walking between the house north of the barn and the road that led down to the rest of the compound. Approaching the barn from the back, she stayed away from the building, hidden in the brush. She moved to get a look at the two guards posted out front. They looked fully alert. She'd been hoping they'd be drowsy, having to stay up all night, but that didn't seem to be the case. Now she had a choice to make. The rotating guard wasn't here, so she must be up at the house, but she would be back in a few minutes.

She could take them both out with the AK-47 quite easily, but that'd be too loud. Trying to get in close and take them down with the knife would work if there was only one. But with two of them, she didn't think she could take down the one and then get to the other before she was shot. The next option would be to pretend that Jezz had sent her and demand to see the prisoners. But that wouldn't work either, unless they were idiots. Max would've prepared those two guards. If she waited for one to nod off or take a leak, she could attack then. However, the whole night could pass with neither moving and then she'd have missed her chance. She may have to try something even riskier.

Cursing silently, she watched as the rotating guard walked down the road toward the barn. The female guard nodded to the guards as she passed, heading for the main compound, and Ana knew she'd be back around in a few minutes.

A noise behind her made her turn, dropping the knife and drawing her Glock. A lone figure crouched a few feet away with NVGs on its head and a combat rifle pointed directly at her. She didn't lower the Glock. Whoever this was knew what they were doing to get this close to her.

"Ana?" the masculine voice whispered. He raised the NVG goggles, showing her a face she thought she'd never see again.

"Emmett?" she asked, holstering her Glock. "I thought they'd killed you!"

He came over and gave her a hug. The gesture surprised her. He hadn't exactly been the affectionate type during their short acquaintance.

"I didn't know if I'd lost you or not," he said, "Is Alexis..."

"She's alive," Ana said, stuffing down the warm feeling rising within her.

Emmett let out a deep breath. "I'd hoped. Why were you walking around freely today?"

"You didn't see?" she asked.

"See what?"

"This morning." She didn't want to tell him. Having Alexis judge her was bad enough.

"No, it took me all night and early morning to find this place. I wasn't up on the ridge watching until noon."

"I..." she began, searching for the right way to put it, "killed Mila to survive in order to rescue your daughter and the others."

The last part hadn't been the whole truth, but it sounded better than her real motives. Emmett seemed to take a second to process it, then looked her dead in the eyes. It was hard to tell in the darkness, but she didn't think she could see any of the judgment she'd seen in Alexis.

"That must have been a hard choice," he said, "but you made the right call. I would've done the same to save my daughter."

She was surprised. Didn't killing Mila make her a monster? Or was Emmett just a monster, too? He was a lot of things but she didn't think he was that. He loved his daughter and would sacrifice anything to save her. Ana felt a little jealous of Alexis in that moment as she wondered what it would be like to have a father like him. Her father hadn't been bad, but he hadn't been like Emmett, either.

"All the adults are inside," Ana said.

"And the children are up in the garage next to the house," Emmett said. "What's your plan?"

"Wait for the sentry to pass, take down the two guards, move inside, and set them free." Then she added as an afterthought. "Then go get the kids."

"Good plan. I'll help you take down the guards, and then I'll go get the kids. I'll meet you back here."

"Alright."

"I'll go around and take the one on the left. You get the right."

Ana nodded and he flipped down his NVG optics, moving off into the night. Within five steps, she'd lost sight of him.

He's good, she thought as she picked up her knife, holstering her Glock.

Moving up to the building, she hung back in the shadows, waiting for the sentry to pass. After another minute, the sentry walked by, nodding to the guards. When she disappeared around the side of the house, Ana moved to the pole barn. She poked her head around and saw a fist showing a thumbs-up on the ground by the other wall. Moving as quickly as she could and staying low, she burst around the side of the building. The guard on the right began to turn to her when his partner grunted and went down with Emmett's knife in the base of his skull. The guard facing Ana started to turn for the closer threat, but it was a mistake. Ana lunged at him as he raised his rifle and plunged her knife into his neck. He twitched and then began to collapse. Emmett caught him, slitting the man's throat on his way to the ground.

"Meet you back here," Emmett said as he took off across the road toward the house, disappearing on the other side.

Ana took a deep breath and opened the door to the barn.

15

ESCAPE

A lexis rested her head against the wooden post. Sleep was evading her. She couldn't get the image of Evan out of her mind—his head bursting and all the contents spraying into the air. She opened her eyes, feeling sick to her stomach, and couldn't decide if the nausea was due to the image or because she hadn't eaten in over twenty-four hours.

How could Ana betray them like this and then act like nothing was wrong? Well, that wasn't entirely true. Alexis had seen some amount of regret in Ana's eyes, but it hadn't been enough to stop her from killing a second time. Once again, Alexis wondered if Ana really had a choice in the matter or if she was just a pawn to Jezz. There was little doubt that maniacal woman was pure evil.

How could Ana do this to me? Alexis asked herself, a tear slipping down her cheek.

She'd only known Ana for a week, but they'd connected. It was like she'd had a sibling again—someone to share the good times with and to help her get through the tough times. Just like when Mason had still been around. A quiet sob escaped her. Mason was dead. Her mother was dead. Ana had betrayed her. James was probably dead. And her dad? She hoped beyond hope that he was still alive. He was the last person she would have left in this world.

Why? she asked God. *Why does this have to happen to good people? How could you let this happen? Where were you when my brother died?*

That last question had haunted her all of her life. The fact that she hadn't been able to do anything as blood filled her brother's lungs as he died still ate at her and had pushed her to pursue a career as a paramedic.

She felt bad for wondering where God had been during her brother's accident. God *had* been there with her, and she distinctly remembered the feeling of peace on those nights when all else seemed lost. Whenever he was home on leave, her dad would come into her room, thinking she was asleep. He'd lie on the floor next to her bed and cry, never knowing she was awake most nights. Even back then she'd known her dad just needed somewhere to let it all out. In the mornings, he was always gone before she awoke and she'd never told him the truth. Those first few months after her brother's death were the only times she could remember seeing her dad cry.

Although it hadn't felt possible at the time, they'd both survived that. It had felt like the world was ending then, but now it truly was. If she could survive that loss, she could survive this. Taking a deep breath, she said a quick prayer and laid her head back again, but she doubted she'd be able to fall asleep. Every time she closed her eyes she either saw Jezz standing over her with that smile on her face or the side of Evan's head exploding.

A noise outside drew her gaze to the door. Shadows were moving under it, cast by the light outside. The door opened and Jezz was standing there, coming back to murder them all. It was like the image in her mind when she closed her eyes, but this was far too real. Fear clenched her throat and she gasped. Jezz rushed into the room, heading straight for her.

Wait—Jezz didn't have bright auburn hair. As Ana crouched down next to her, Alexis breathed easier. It'd just been her frayed mind playing tricks on her.

"Look," Ana said, a pair of keys in her blood covered hand, "I know you don't like me right now. But let's get out of here, and then—"

"Are you crazy?" Alexis said. "I'm not going anywhere with you! This is just a setup—"

"Shut up," Ana growled, shocking her with the ferocity in her voice. "Your dad is here with me. We don't have time for this."

Her dad—alive? Ana moved in to unchain her but Alexis turned, blocking her from getting to the shackles.

"You're lying," Alexis said.

Ana roughly grabbed her by the shoulder and turned her so she could get at the shackles. Alexis wanted to head-butt her but decided against it. Even if this was all a ruse, she could still use this chance to get away. The key clicked in the lock and the shackles fell off her wrists. She tried to bring her arms in front of her, but her muscles ached in protest. Rubbing her wrists, she looked up at Ana, anger burning in her eyes.

"If you're lying to me..." Alexis said.

"Get over yourself," Ana said. "I'm here to rescue you."

Alexis stood up shakily, leaning on the wooden post behind her. She pointed at Ana, who was about to move away.

"Get over myself? Ana, you murdered two people just to save your own skin!"

"My *own* skin?" Ana asked, her anger boiling over. "I did it to save *your* skin!"

Alexis was taken aback, not only by the raw anger but by the words. Ana had done it for her? Before she could respond, Ana stomped off to Beverly and began to unlock her shackles. This was really happening. She'd come back to rescue them, but how did her father come into this? Alexis followed Ana.

"Give me the keys," Alexis said. When Ana glared at her, she explained. "I'll free everyone while you guard the door. Or give me a gun and I will."

Ana finished with Beverly's shackles and then shoved the keys into Alexis's hand.

"You better hurry," Ana said as she walked away. "They'll discover the bodies soon."

Alexis ignored the questions that rose in her mind and moved to unchain Greg.

"Thanks," he said. "I may have been wrong to argue with you."

Alexis nodded to him. She wasn't in the mood to talk right now. Within a few minutes, she had them all free and moved over to the door where Ana was standing just inside the shadows.

"Do you have a gun I can use?" Alexis asked.

Without turning to her, Ana pulled a handgun from behind her back and gave it to her, along with an extra magazine. Alexis looked down, using the light from the open doorway to study the gun. It was a Glock. Her dad had had her shoot one when he'd trained her all those years ago.

"I'm sorry," Alexis said. "I thought—"

"Save it," Ana said, cutting her off. "Let's survive the night. Then the debt will be paid."

There was an edge to Ana's voice, not that Alexis could blame her. If Ana had really done all this for her, then Alexis had acted like a world-class jerk. But the fact that Ana had killed Mila and Evan still rubbed her wrong. Even if her motives had been right, would it change the fact that she'd taken two lives to save one? Alexis didn't know the answer to that, but she was glad it hadn't been her decision to make because there was no way she would have been able to do what Ana had done.

The rest of the survivors had all moved to the doorway now. Greg was at the front of the group and had chains from the shackles wrapped around his hand. He caught Alexis looking at them.

"If we have to fight, I want to have some kind of weapon," Greg said.

"Here they come," Ana said, leaving the doorway and stepping outside.

Alexis followed. She looked up to see her dad coming down the road with all the children behind him. She had to use all her self-control not to go running into his arms like a little girl, but that didn't stop the huge smile spreading on her face. Her dad was alive, and by the looks of it, mostly uninjured. He had a few cuts on his face and arms. When he saw her, his pace picked up and the kids had to jog to stay with him. He didn't slow until he was right in front of her. Then he dropped his rifle and wrapped his arms around her.

She was shocked by the abandon with which he hugged her. It was almost crushing. Holding back tears, she returned the hug. He must've been worried sick about her to act like this. Her heart felt like bursting and in her dad's embrace, the whole world slipped away. She was safe and secure, even with everything falling apart around them. As long as her dad was around, she would be able to get through whatever the world threw at her.

"I thought I'd lost you," Emmett said, his voice husky.

"Me too," Alexis said with tears in her eyes.

Emmett gently pushed her back to an arm's length, looking her in the eyes. "I love you, honey. Whatever happens, know that I'll always love you."

"And I love you, daddy."

Emmett chuckled. "Enough of this emotional stuff. We should probably leave now."

"Probably," Alexis said, smiling. Even though he acted tough, she knew better.

"Were there any vehicles up there?" Ana asked.

"Only a small car," Emmett said, picking up his discarded rifle. "We can go out the way I came in, over the hills."

"Do you have a vehicle to fit us all?" Beverly asked. "You can't expect all these kids to follow on foot."

Emmett glanced at the children. "The only other option is going down into the compound for transportation, but there's no way we can get out without a fight."

"The kids won't make it on foot," Greg said.

"Then we go down into the compound," Emmett said. "Pair up into groups of eight—two adults and six kids. An adult from each pair will go for a rig, the bigger the better."

"I can go ahead and check for keys," Ana said.

"Good plan," Emmett said. "Now, everyone else pair up and follow me."

"Where's Mila?" Olive asked from among the children.

Alexis had forgotten that the girl had been close to Mila. She walked over to her and bent down.

"Hi, Olive," Alexis said.

"Hey, Alexis," Olive said, smiling, but her smile began to fade as the little girl looked into Alexis's eyes.

"Mila... didn't make it. Did she?" Olive said.

"I'm so sorry, sweetie," Alexis said with tears in her eyes.

Tears began to pool in Olive's eyes.

"We need to go, honey," Emmett said, resting a hand on Alexis's shoulder.

With a sniffle and a swipe of her sleeve, Olive looked at Alexis. "I'll be okay."

Felix walked up and rested a protective hand on Olive's shoulder. "I'll stick with her and make sure nothing happens," he said, looking up at Emmett. Alexis noticed he had a black eye and some bruising on his arms.

"You're a good kid," Emmett said. "Now go get with Greg's group and do as he says."

"Yes, sir," Felix said, steering Olive away.

The last glance Olive gave Alexis almost broke her heart. The little girl was so strong. Even in the midst of this, she was holding it together. She was stronger than most of the adults were.

"Alexis," Emmett said, "bring up the rear and make sure no one falls behind."

"Yes, sir," Alexis said, falling back into her role.

She was safe and her dad was alive. They were going to get out of this. In retrospect, they hadn't lost as many as they could have. They just had to survive the night and they'd be back on the road.

Emmett looked at them one last time. They'd all paired up. There were three groups of two adults with six kids and one group of five adults, plus Alexis bringing up the rear. The kids were holding up surprisingly well. Maybe they could tell the stakes were high, or maybe they were just getting used to this, but for some reason they were all silent as they slipped through the night. He didn't know why and didn't spend much time thinking about it. They were ready.

"You five," Emmett said to the group of adults, "stay in front and be ready to help. If I hold up a closed fist, that means stop. If I motion forward, that means come up. Got it?" He waited until he received various forms of confirmation. "Good. We're movin' out."

Flipping his NVGs down, Emmett started at a quick pace down the road toward the main compound. Ana would have had a few minutes to find the best vehicles to commandeer. Judging by the lack of gunshots, she hadn't been discovered. Yet. There was always the possibility that at any second they could be in a fight for their lives. Every moment they stayed there lowered their chances of surviving.

As they neared the main compound, Emmett held up a closed fist and the others obediently stopped behind him. He continued forward in a crouch, stopping just off the road out of the light from the various porch lights and other outdoor lights, where he waited for Ana. The wait wasn't long. Less than a minute later, Ana came running toward him in a half crouch.

"They only have four that are unlocked with the keys in them," Ana said. "One is your truck, but James's is locked."

"Perfect, we'll take them all," Emmett said as they went back to the rest of the group. "Listen up. We don't want to put the kids in the line of fire. I need one adult from each group and whoever else wants to help. The rest of you take the kids down the driveway as far as you can. It'll meet up at the road, and if you get that far, stop there. We'll come with the vehicles."

"I'll come with you," Greg said, "although I could use a gun."

Emmett slung the black bag off of his back and unzipped it, handing Greg the other rifle. Beverly and Troy, the redhead, stepped up and he gave them each one of his extra handguns. Ana gave Lucas the Glock holstered on her hip.

"Lucas and Alexis," Emmett said, "go with the kids and make sure they're protected. The rest of you come with me."

Emmett moved off with Ana right next to him. The three armed survivors and four drivers—Todd, Seth, Abby, and Mark—followed while the rest of the group headed down the driveway. Ana pointed out the four vehicles to the drivers.

One of the RVs lit up from inside and someone opened the door. The man stepped out, stretching, followed by another man.

"Hey, Dave," the lead man called toward the small house, "time to switch."

He started walking over to the door while a woman also climbed out of the RV.

"They can't go inside," Ana hissed. "They'll find the bodies."

"Roger," Emmett said, looking at the four drivers. "When we take down those three, make a run to the rigs, get them started, and get out of here. We'll follow."

They nodded.

"Hey, Dave!" the lead man said, knocking on the door to the house.

The sound of a gunshot broke the silence and the man crumpled to the ground, staining the door crimson. Emmett fired immediately after Ana, taking down the woman who'd honed in on their location. Greg took down the third. The four drivers burst from cover, running toward the line of vehicles. Lights came on in all the RVs and people started shouting.

"Get ready," Emmett said.

One of the RV doors began to open and Emmett put a couple rounds into it. He heard glass shattering from the RV where the three had come from originally. Someone had the barrel of a rifle sticking out one of the windows and they fired, hitting Todd as he ran for the vehicles. Ana returned fire, taking down the Reclaimer who'd shot. The three other drivers made it to the vehicles and scrambled inside. Todd was still on the ground with blood covering his back. He was dead.

"Someone grab that black Ford!" Emmett said, firing on one of the RVs where someone had tried to shoot from a window.

"On it!" Troy said, running for Emmett's truck.

Emmett was laying down covering fire on the RV with the most activity when gunfire sounded from behind them. He turned around. Six Reclaimers were running toward them from the house north of the driveway, firing as they ran. Emmett returned fire, taking down two before they dodged for cover. All of the drivers had their vehicles started and were pulling out. They sped past Emmett and his small group, turning down the driveway and heading toward the road. Troy shortly followed the rest, driving Emmett's truck.

"We need to go!" Emmett yelled.

The others took off running across the dirt road and into the darkness on the other side. The Reclaimers from up by the house fired on them, but they couldn't get a bead. Emmett turned around and laid down some covering fire, then ran after them. After a minute, they'd arrived at the vehicles and the last of the kids were loaded in. One of the trucks was a single cab and had been hit with a round. Smoke was leaking from under the hood.

"We'll need to leave that one," Alexis said, coming up to them. "We loaded the extra people into the bed of our truck. We got all the kids inside."

"Good," Emmett said. "Greg, Beverly, get in the bed of this last truck. Ana—"

"I'll take the smoking truck and head toward the interstate," Ana said. "I'll draw them off, then join up with you."

"Ana," Alexis began.

"There's no time to argue," Ana said. "I'll meet up with you at the Canadian border."

The girls shared a look. Ana was determined to do this, Emmett could tell. Something like understanding crossed Alexis's face and she was about to say something, but the sound of approaching engines stopped her, forcing them into action.

"Okay," Emmett said. "Alexis, tell the drivers to head east, and after a bit, have them turn their lights off. Now let's move!"

Beverly and Greg loaded up and Alexis took off to inform the drivers.

"Good luck," Emmett said, giving Ana a quick hug before going to the last truck and climbing into the bed with the other two.

Ana waved at him and then climbed into the smoking truck. The caravan took off with Ana in the rear. When they reached the road, they took a right while Ana turned left and then slowed the truck. She would wait to see the Reclaimers before taking off toward the interstate. Hopefully, their ruse would work and they wouldn't be chased. Or at the very least they could get some distance between them.

The caravan started to climb a hill and the drivers turned off their lights, slowing down. They continued to drive over the hill. At the crest, Emmett looked down to the driveway and saw that Ana had her truck moving. A set of headlights shone from the driveway. The Reclaimers had taken the bait. Emmett lost sight of them when the truck started its descent. Hopefully, the decoy would work. Either way, Ana would be on her own now. She was a resourceful woman though; she'd make it to the border. She might even meet up with James and Connor somewhere, if they were still alive. Their caravan continued on into the night, farther from the Reclaimers and closer to safety with each passing minute.

16

MISSING

J ames stood in the dark pole barn. This had to be where the Reclaimers were keeping their group. The poles with chains and
shackles were enough to prove that, but where were they now? Had
they killed them all or moved them to a different location?

"The gunfire," Connor stated.

"They broke out," James said, turning.

"Time to get down there and help out, then!" Tank said.

Connor took the lead and James followed, with Tank behind him.
As James left the barn, he couldn't help but wonder who'd been killed.
He'd noticed a dark stain in front of one of the posts but tried not
to dwell on it. He knew he couldn't change anything at this point,
but that didn't stop his mind from running in a hundred different
directions. Selfishly, he hoped Alexis was alive still, and Mila and
Olive—especially little Olive.

They left the barn behind and started down the road to the main
collection of buildings. The gunfire had died down and some vehicles
had moved off. Multiple engines roared to life, and there was yelling
between the buildings and the RVs.

Movement to their right caught his eye. James's IR laser settled on
the Reclaimer just as his brother's laser shone on the man. His brother
fired. The man was hit in the chest and James fired a round just to

make sure he was down for good. The man collapsed, the suppressed shots going unheard amid all the other noises. James searched behind where the man had been, the landscape cast in a green hue from his night vision.

"Clear," James said.

"Clear behind," Tank said.

"Movin' on," Connor said.

They continued on their way, more wary than before. It seemed that not all the Reclaimers were down by the commotion. Four sets of taillights headed down the driveway as a woman with black hair continued shouting and people piled into the last two vehicles. When they were full, she climbed into a silver SUV and they took off down the driveway, red taillights swallowed by the darkness.

Slowly, they neared the main collection of buildings, moving off the road and into the shadows. James flipped up his NVGs as they neared the buildings since all the lights were making them ineffective.

Coming around the back side of another barn, they looked to where all the RVs were parked in a semi-circle. Only two vehicles remained—a small car with bullet holes and a broken windshield, and an old truck that probably wouldn't even start. All of the other vehicles they'd seen from the hill were gone. Only two Reclaimers remained that they could see. The two men were walking over to the small house.

"I can't believe they just left us here," one of the men said.

"Someone has to hold down the fort," the other replied.

"Take them alive," Connor said, aiming through his scope now that his NVGs were up.

"Roger," James said.

From a kneeling position at maybe thirty yards, it wouldn't be a hard shot. He waited for his brother to shoot first. Connor fired and the man on the right screamed out, clutching his leg. James breathed out and squeezed the trigger as the second man began to turn. The sixty-two-grain 5.56mm bullet tore through the man's thigh. He didn't go down, however, and James had to shoot him through his other leg before he collapsed.

"Tank, stay on 'em. If they move, tear 'em in half," Connor said.

"With pleasure," Tank said, resting the SAW on a fencepost.

Connor, followed shortly by James, moved from the shadows into the light. The first man on the ground made a move for his rifle.

"Don't even think about it!" Tank yelled at him.

The man stilled, looking toward them. The other man was in too much pain to worry about his shotgun. He'd been shot in the right thigh and left kneecap. James went up to the second man while his brother went to the other. Kicking away his shotgun, he quickly looked him over for another weapon but didn't see one.

"You armed?" James said.

"You shot me!" the man said, teeth clenched.

"Yes," James said, "and I'll shoot you again if you don't start answering my questions."

"Okay, what do you want?"

"Are you armed?"

"No."

"Good. Now, what happened here?"

"Those damn captives got loose and started shooting us."

"Where'd they go?"

"Down the road, probably toward the interstate."

"You're the only two they left behind?"

"Yes, just us."

"How many more are there?"

"Hell, I don't know now. We lost a lot. There's maybe two dozen of us left."

"Thanks for your cooperation."

"What are you going to do with me now?"

"Not sure."

James glanced over at Connor as he talked to the other Reclaimer.

"I won't tell you—" the man was cut off when a bullet entered his brain.

"Idiot," Connor said, walking over to James. "You get what we need?"

"Yep," James said.

"Please spare me," the man James had shot begged.

Connor walked up to the other man and shot him in the head. James felt some remorse. That hadn't been completely necessary, but he wasn't going to say anything. The man would have died soon anyway with wounds like that. Even if he had lived, what kind of life would it be without the use of his legs in the apocalypse? It was easier this way.

"Let's take this," James said, going to the shot-up blue compact car.

"Tank, we're rollin' out," Connor said.

Tank came running out of the shadows just as James settled into the driver's seat. Connor and Tank ducked in as the car started and James stepped on the gas. The car lurched forward only a few feet and then began to make funny noises. Pedal to the floor, it topped out at about two miles per hour.

"Umm... I think we'd be faster crawlin'," Tank said.

"Yeah..." James said, putting the car in park.

They bailed out, starting to jog down the driveway to the road. Once out of the light, James flipped down his NVGs. The others followed suit and they continued, leaving the Reclaimers' hideout behind. A couple of minutes later, they arrived at the red gravel road. James looked down, trying to see if he could guess which way they'd gone. The most recent marks did seem to be going to the left, toward the interstate, but it could be that he was just seeing what he wanted to.

"Which way?" Tank asked.

"Hell, I don't know," James said. "But if I had to guess, I'd say they went left."

"Makes the most sense," Connor said.

"Let's go get Chloe then head after 'em," James said, as they started down the road.

After a few minutes of jogging, Tank spoke up. "You do realize we don't have to run."

"I'm glad someone said it," James said, out of breath. "I was about to die."

"Me too," Connor said, breathing heavily. "I just didn't want to be the first."

"I decided to use my brain instead of my pride," Tank said.

"Good thing someone did," James said.

"This kinda sucks," Tank said.

"What does?" James asked.

"We didn't get to rescue anyone with all our new gear," Tank said.

"It *was* very anti-climactic," Connor said.

"I envisioned us rollin' in and kickin' ass and takin' names," Tank said.

"Me too," James said.

"So what happens if we don't find 'em?" Tank asked as they walked.

"We continue north," James said. "Our best bet is that we'll find them at the Canadian border. Emmett, Alexis, and Ana all know the plan. They'll expect us to pass through Sweet Grass."

"And if they aren't there?" Tank asked.

"Then we continue north anyway," James said.

"What about your truck?" Connor asked. "It has all our gear."

James winced. He'd been trying not to think about that, and with all that was going on, he'd been doing a good job, but now it was in the forefront of his mind. It honestly felt like he'd lost a friend, not knowing where his truck was or if it had been shot up. Not only was it a nice truck, but it held all of their remaining earthly possessions. That happened to mostly be guns, ammunition, and food, as well as their clothing, backpacks, and other gear. Not to mention their iPods. Those were even more important. How were they supposed to get all that music back if their iPods were gone? There was no more Cloud or iTunes. They'd have lost a huge part of their lives. Okay, that was a little dramatic, even just saying it in his head. But if all their stuff was gone, he would miss his music the most.

"I was trying not to think about that," James said.

"Oh, sorry bro," Connor said. "I know you get attached to things."

"You're telling me you don't miss your other guns?" James asked.

"A little, but I have my AR back in the Hummer," Connor said. "Plus, we have these new ones, and I'm really diggin' it."

"I am, too," Tank said, "But if I keep luggin' it around all the time, I'd better get to shoot someone soon. If not, I'm gonna get one of those light numbers you have."

"They *are* more practical," James said.

"Oh, you and your practicality," Tank said.

"What? Is it bad I think like that?" James asked.

"Yes," Tank said. "Live a little, be impractical."

"That'll just get me killed," James said.

"I don't mean with something survival-wise," Tank said. "Just let your hair down every once in a while. Go out with your heels on."

"Uh... I don't have hair or a pair of heels," James said.

"Sure ya don't," Tank said. "We all know you're a cross-dresser."

"You're ridiculous," James said.

"Don't we know that, Connor?" Tank asked.

"Of course," Connor said. "Those late nights with you standing in front of a mirror with your red dress and lipstick on."

"Oh, *those* nights," James said, sarcastically. "I remember those nights."

"See?" Tank said.

"You mean those nights that *never* happened?" James said.

"Keep denying it," Tank said. "It just makes you all the guiltier."

Connor and Tank chuckled.

James just shook his head. Those two were always picking on him, even back in school. Most of the time James just laughed along and brushed it off; however, sometimes they prodded a little too hard and hit a nerve. When that happened, he reacted, so they kept doing it to get that reaction. Not tonight, though, because this joking was a little too far-fetched and he knew its purpose was mostly to keep all their minds off of what lay ahead.

They needed to catch up to a group of twenty-some armed killers who were chasing their friends. Then, they'd either have to kill the Reclaimers or sneak around them. That was if they could find either group. They may be going in the completely wrong direction or the Reclaimers could catch them first and finish them off. Tonight they'd had the element of surprise. If the Reclaimers set up another ambush, they'd catch them with their pants down. If they couldn't find their group, they'd have to continue north without his truck or their gear.

The only thing that gave them the upper hand was the guns and gear they'd found on the hilltop.

Finally, after what seemed like hours with all their gear on and little sleep for the past couple of days, they arrived at the base of the hill. Climbing up the side, they reached the top, out of breath. They walked past the first pavilion.

"Hey, guys, I'll be right out," Tank said, heading inside. "I want to see if I can find anythin' that explains what's going on. Meet you at the Hummer."

"Sounds good," James said.

They continued on to the Hummer that was parked by the last pavilion. The vehicle was empty, with the back door open. Going around to the back, James stopped. All the gear they'd collected was gone. No Chloe and no gear.

"Really?" Connor asked, looking in the Hummer. "Again?"

James quickly went around to the front and opened the door. Chloe was definitely gone, along with everything inside. He moved into the pavilion to see whether she'd moved it for some reason, but everything was as they'd left it—personal effects untouched, all the useful gear taken. Running now, he entered the middle pavilion. This one was even emptier now than when they'd left it. Someone had definitely been there and they'd taken more supplies. He walked into the last pavilion. Tank was looking through the paperwork scattered around.

"Hey, buddy," James said.

"What's wrong now?" Tank asked. "You have that tone in your voice."

"All of our gear's gone," James said, "and Chloe is missing."

17

ON THE ROAD AGAIN

Post-outbreak day 8, morning

A lexis sat in the passenger's seat of her dad's truck, watching the sunrise out the window. Sunlight reflected off the Tongue River Reservoir, making the water glisten. They'd driven through the early morning, not daring to stop so close to the Reclaimers base. If Ana failed and the Reclaimers doubled back, it wouldn't be good if they'd stopped only a few miles away. Now, they were north of Decker, Montana, on MT-314. Staying off the interstate had been challenging since she didn't know which way to go. Luckily, Troy knew the area relatively well and was navigating so they wouldn't hit the interstate until I-94, somewhere near Colstrip.

She glanced back at the five sleeping kids shoved into the back seat and then over at Troy. He'd really stepped up after their time in the pole barn. She hadn't even known his name before because he stayed in the background. Then, after their talk, he'd volunteered to help get the vehicles and then went for her dad's truck after Todd had been shot. She felt a pang of sadness, knowing Todd wasn't alive anymore. They were losing so many. In just the past two days, they'd gone from a hundred and fourteen when they'd first rescued them from the elementary school to now only twenty-eight.

This was really taking its toll on them. Then again, it was the end of the world. Or was it? She'd been thinking about that a lot lately.

If they could get to Alaska and really do what they planned, it would be the start of a new life. The Earth would continue on, and by that definition this wasn't the end of the world. It was just another bloody, gruesome chapter in human history.

She glanced in the rearview mirror, wanting to see James's white truck following them. She missed those two, but if she was honest with herself, she missed James more. When had that happened? She'd always felt connected to both of the brothers because they reminded her of her brother, but now James was in her mind more, and she found herself worrying about him. Had they survived the ambush? Or had they given their lives to help them escape? She prayed they were safe, but there was no way to know for sure. They could both be walking corpses by now. Yet, she had to hope they were still out there and would meet up with them soon.

"When are you wantin' to stop and regroup?" Troy asked, glancing at her.

"Soon. We should be far enough away for a quick stop," Alexis responded.

"How about up there?" Troy asked.

A half a mile in front of them on the west side of the road was a large coal mine with a dirt road leading down into it. They'd be out of sight down there, and if the Reclaimers were following them, they'd slip right by.

"That's perfect," Alexis said.

"Sweet," Troy said.

They turned off on the road and headed down into the strip mine. Layer upon layer of dirt had been removed to find the black treasure buried beneath. Continuing, they drove down into one of the large pits. There were a few infected roaming around, but nothing they couldn't handle. Troy pulled the truck to a stop and Alexis got out, grabbing the machete her dad kept wedged between the passenger seat and center console. Three infected were coming their way, while another four were going for the other vehicles pulling in behind her. Walking up to the first one, she swung the machete. The blade smashed into its skull and it collapsed to the ground. The impact from the blow reverberated through her hand and up her arm. Hitting a hard object with another object hurt. The second one walked up and she swung again, aiming for its eye this time. The skull was weaker there and the machete did more damage without hurting her as much. The third arrived quicker than she'd anticipated and she had to rush her swing. It didn't have as much force but was enough to drop the zombie. As it lay on the ground, she stabbed it through the eye just to be safe.

"That was impressive," Troy said, walking up to her. "I was ready to step in and play the hero, but you took care of them all by yourself. You're a remarkable woman."

"Thanks," Alexis said, smiling.

Emmett walked over to her, having taken care of the other infected. The rest of the group climbed out of the vehicles and began to stretch. The ones shoved into the back of her dad's truck seemed relieved to finally be out of the cramped space. Luckily for them, the mattresses had still been laid out in the bed of the truck.

"Good job, honey," Emmett said.

"Thanks, daddy," Alexis said, teasing.

Her dad smiled and pulled her into a hug. "I love you, Alexis. I would've been lost without you."

Pulling away, he looked into her eyes and she smiled, tearing up. Her dad had been worried sick about her. She could see that by the relief in his eyes. There seemed to even be a few tears welling up in them. He would never let them show—he was too strong for that—but they were there nonetheless. She was the luckiest girl in the world to have a dad who cared about her this much. As she thought about it, she could look back in her past and see he'd always cared about her. He'd always told her she was his first priority in life after the divorce, but given the emotional state she'd been in then, she hadn't believed him. How could someone mean that when they constantly left? Now, with all they were going through, she was beginning to realize firsthand that serving in the corps was the ultimate way to show her how much he loved her. She only wished she'd realized it before.

"Okay, everyone," Emmett said, raising his voice so the whole group could hear. "We need to figure out how many more vehicles we need. My daughter and I will fit in my truck, along with Olive, Felix, and two other kids, comfortably. What about the others?"

"I can fit myself and another adult in the minivan," Abby said, "plus six to eight kids."

"We've got room for two adults and four or five kids," Seth said. "My two daughters will stay with me."

"We need at least one more vehicle then," Greg said, "Two to be comfortable."

Emmett nodded. "Okay, I'm going to see what gear I still have. Then I'll take Greg, Lucas, and Troy with me to go check out the house across the road. Everyone else stay close to the vehicles and be ready to leave."

"What if we need to go pee?" one of the little boys asked.

"Go behind the truck and piss," Emmett said.

"Outside?" the little boy asked.

"You've never gone outside?" Emmett asked.

He shook his head.

"What's your name?" Alexis asked.

"Eli," the boy said.

"And how old are you Eli?"

"Six," he said with a slight lisp.

Alexis felt her heart melting. The little guy was so cute with his short blonde hair, blue eyes, and lopsided smile.

"Hey, Eli," Troy said, walking up to him. "I'll show you. C'mon."

"Okay," Eli said, perking up.

The two of them walked out of sight on the other side of the truck.

Helen walked up. "His father died right before he was born and his mother raised him," she said.

"Where's his mother now?" Emmett asked.

"She never showed up at the school," Helen said. "A lot of the parents never did."

"If anyone else has to use the bathroom, just find a spot and go," Emmett said to the gathered kids and adults. "If you need to shi—go number two, then ask an adult and maybe we can find some toilet paper."

Alexis followed her dad as he walked over to the bed of his truck and climbed in, searching.

"Looks like they left my duffle of clothes, the mattresses, and sleeping bags. They took all the food, water, ammo, and guns," Emmett said with a sigh.

Alexis walked over to the back seat and looked underneath, hoping maybe they'd missed it. They hadn't. The food, ammunition, and couple of extra handguns were all missing. The Reclaimers had taken everything they needed and left the rest. She walked back around to the bed as her dad was closing the tailgate.

"Nothing," Alexis said.

"I assumed," Emmett said. "It could be worse, I guess. The main thing is, you're safe and I got my truck back."

He walked around to where most of the group was still gathered in hushed conversation. "You guys ready?" he asked.

"Yeah," Greg said as he walked over, hoisting his rifle.

Lucas and Troy followed, each carrying the handgun they'd been given, and the three of them loaded into Emmett's truck. Emmett walked over to Alexis and stopped in front of her, staring. She could tell he wanted to say something, probably about how much he loved her and that if anything happened, it'd be okay.

"I know, Dad," Alexis said, smiling. "You'll be back soon."

"You always could see right through me," Emmett said. He gave her a quick hug. "I'll see you soon, sweetie."

"See you soon, Dad," Alexis said.

Her dad climbed into his truck and turned it around, driving out of the large pit.

Emmett watched his daughter in the rearview mirror as Olive came up to her and Alexis bent down to hug her. He could only imagine what Olive was going through right then. She'd lost her aunt, then her aunt's friend who was taking care of her, and now Mila. That'd be tough for a kid, but Olive seemed to be handling it well. He returned his attention to driving.

"This is a nice truck," Troy said. "Did you do all these upgrades?"

"Yeah," Emmett said. He wanted to like Troy, but he was almost too likable, and that irritated him.

"Bars on the windows, the brush guard, shooting bench, and is this bulletproof glass?" Greg asked.

"Yeah, the body is bulletproof, too."

"It almost seems like you were prepared for this," Greg said.

"I was," Emmett said. "I like to be prepared for anything. After my years in the corps, I decided to take precautions in case anything happened."

Emmett glanced over at him. While Greg might not have meant anything by it, Emmett had picked up on something in Greg's voice. Greg faced forward, not looking at him.

"Good thing," Greg said.

"Yeah," Troy said. "It really helped us out."

Emmett nodded.

He was beginning to dislike both men for two completely different reasons. He found himself wishing James and Connor were here. When he was around those two, it was easy to see how unhinged and dangerous they were. But when compared to these people, he would gladly take the brothers in any state. If they could just get a grip on their emotions, they'd work like a well-oiled machine. Thinking about them made him think about his own brother. If he had Alex here with him, they'd be unstoppable, just like those early years in the corps. How he wished he could have his brother back. His mind strayed down the path it always did when he started to think about him. He'd not only lost his brother but his marriage as well and... Mason.

They arrived at the highway just then and Emmett buried those thoughts. No time to think about his failures in life now. He drove across the highway and down the driveway to the house they'd seen. Slowing, he stopped by the house. There were three vehicles parked out front.

"That doesn't look very promising," Lucas said.

"No, it doesn't," Troy said.

The three vehicles looked like they'd been sitting there for years, and the house looked the same. Part of the roof had caved in and a tarp was tied over it. Some of the windows were missing glass and plywood now covered them. Either this house hadn't been lived in for years or the person living there had very little money to spend on renovations.

"Stay frosty," Emmett said, getting out of the truck. "We don't know what's around here."

The rest climbed out. Emmett walked over to the vehicles and inspected them more closely. If they even started, they wouldn't make it more than five miles down the road. On the other end of the house was a large, makeshift shed made up of different pieces of sheet metal. The entrance had a tarp strapped over it and the edges blew in the gusting wind, making a snapping sound. With the ACR to his shoulder, Emmett approached cautiously. Greg kept an eye on the house while Lucas and Troy checked the other vehicles scattered in the field. They'd have no luck there. All of them looked like rusty shells rather than actual working vehicles.

The tarp blew in a gust, showing Emmett the inside, and his pulse spiked. They hadn't seen him yet and somehow hadn't heard the truck pull up, probably because of the wind. Backing up slowly, he kept his eyes forward.

"Hey, Emmett!" Troy yelled. "We might have something!"

Emmett cursed under his breath as the infecteds' heads snapped toward the noise.

"Get ready!" Emmett yelled. "We have company!"

The first infected stumbled past the tarp and out into the sunlight. With the reticle of his scope settling on its head, he pulled the trigger. The suppressed gunshot cracked and its head snapped back. Before the first body hit the ground, he'd fired again, taking down another. Four more poured from the exit and Emmett continued to fire as he slowly backed up. Two more hit the ground, but now there were eight of them coming at him from the makeshift building.

"The house!" Greg yelled as he ran toward the truck.

Out of the corner of his eye, Emmett caught sight of Greg stopping and shooting at the house as four infected poured from a hole in the side. Lucas and Troy were behind Greg, trying to shoot them with the handguns, and failing. They were over twenty yards away—not an easy shot for the untrained.

A dozen infected shambled toward Emmett from the makeshift building. "Get to the truck!" he yelled, shooting once more and then turning.

He sprinted for the truck. Lucas and Troy were almost there. Looking back, he found that three infected were almost on Greg. He stopped and aimed at them. With three quick shots, they were down and Greg was at the truck. Sensing the horde closing in on him, Emmett spun around. An infected reached for him only a few inches from the end of his barrel. It took a round in the face and so did the next one. He took a quick step back, tripping on a rock. Falling to his back, the wind was knocked from his lungs. He leaned forward, aiming at the remaining creatures that were closing in on him. Two were already at his feet. He shot one in the head but the other fell to its knees, grabbing his leg.

18

CONSEQUENCES

C hloe sat in the Hummer, her thoughts matching the darkness outside. She'd known in her heart they'd only have one chance to get free and that it would have to be her, but she couldn't tell the others. It needed to be believable. Bryce may have been a little crazy, but he was smart and suspicious. The plan had just fallen into place and she'd gone with it. Pulling the trigger hadn't been the hard part; watching Bryce die had been. That was part of the reason she'd shot him in the head. She couldn't stand to see him suffer, and she'd fled as soon as she could. It was the first time she'd killed anything.

Now she sat there, her mind not allowing her to rest. She needed to see him again. Slipping the handgun into her pocket, she climbed out of the Hummer. Going around to the back, she opened it, grabbing one of the helmets from a bag. It took her a minute but she finally figured out how to turn the night vision on. With the helmet secure on her head, handgun in her pocket, and looking at the world through a green filter, she went back into the pavilion. In the little corner room, still lying on the bed, was the body. She approached him, her heart pounding in her chest.

I did that, she thought. *I killed him. Ended a life.*

Bile rose in her throat. How could she have done that? Looking down at him, she found herself feeling sorry for him. He'd threatened them and kept them hostage, but he'd never hurt them. Yet, she'd killed him. Didn't even hesitate. Without even thinking, she'd grabbed the gun, pointed it at him, and pulled the trigger. Now he was dead, lying in a pool of his own congealed blood.

"I'm sorry," Chloe whispered. "I didn't want to do it, but I had to. We had to get free. I'm so sorry."

She began to cry. His blood was on her hands and she'd never be able to wash it off. She'd taken a life. Sitting down at the foot of his cot, she pulled her helmet off and let the tears flow freely. She cried for Bryce, who hadn't deserved to die, for her parents who were probably dead, and for herself. Most of all she cried for herself. Her whole life she'd tried to do what was right, not because of some religion telling her she had to, but because she wanted to—helping people, being nice, caring, and loving. Yet she'd always had a hard time doing it. Most people annoyed her and she always had a retort for them. Her parents had never been the nice type, and her dad used to tell her, "Trust no one. They'll always disappoint you." It wasn't until years later she'd realized how far that was from the truth, but it was hard for her to fight her natural instincts. To top it all off, she'd just shot someone.

Sometime later, her tears began to dry up. Wiping them away, she stood and picked up her discarded helmet. She had to do something to get her mind off of this. Flipping the NVGs down, she looked around, and something on a box next to Bryce's cot caught her attention. It was a small leather book. She picked it up and looked at the front page. It was his personal journal. There were dates going all the way back to the first of the year and all the way up to tonight. Going out to the Hummer, she climbed into the driver's seat and turned the dome light on.

She flipped to the earliest entry.

January 2nd

New Year's resolution. I'll quit drinking. He wouldn't have wanted me to mourn him this way. He was too young to die. He only had twelve years. My little Elliot. He would have been ashamed of me. I can't have that. I'll stop drinking and maybe even go see a shrink.

She flipped forward a few pages.

April 23ʳᵈ

I'm still hearing his voice. What has it been now, six months? It seems like I lost him just yesterday. The shrink says it's part of the normal bereavement stage. But I responded to him the other day and we held a conversation for five whole minutes! You can't tell me that's normal. I'm also starting to see him. Not directly, just out of the corner of my eye. Oh, Allie, how I wish you were still here. You would know just what to do.

She skipped ahead.

June 1ˢᵗ

My shrink was right. I just need to accept this as normal. Now everything is like it was. I have my son back. We talk constantly and he follows me around everywhere I go, except to work, of course, I put a movie on for him. He loves How to Train Your Dragon *and he's still watching it when I get back. Work is getting tougher. It's just so hard to be away from him now. But that'll all change soon. I put in to move to a field unit, and since those guys do nothing but train anyway, I'll have more time to be home. I don't know why they want an analyst anyway, but it pays better and will be more flexible. I'll just need to be ready for the call that won't ever come.*

She turned to the last page. It had two entries on it.

June 30th

We captured some survivors today. Not sure if they're part of the other group or not. They seem different, not as violent. Elliot likes the girl, says she reminds him of mom. Not sure what we're going to do with them. We want to trust them, but we know better. We'll think on it, but we know what way we're leaning. Nothing can compromise the mission. We have to recover everything. The boss won't be happy if we don't find everything and everyone. I just finished burying Gary out back last night.

We can't trust the three, only Chloe. She is nice and we like her. She can stay. We have to kill the others. We need to come up with a way so she doesn't suspect us. Maybe poison their food? No, if she eats some of theirs, she'll die. We can't have that. Elliot needs a mother to help raise him. There aren't many eligible women left. We just need to come up with a way. We'll sleep on it and decide in the morning. We'll do it tomorrow.

Chloe closed the journal, tucking it under her arm. She felt somewhat better now. Yes, Bryce was tormented by the death of his son, but he'd been planning to kill the guys and take her as his wife. She still felt bad for him and horrible about herself, but she'd acted and it'd saved her friends. That was all she needed to know.

Turning the dome light off, she tossed the journal into the passenger's seat. She stared out the windshield, the moonlight reflecting off something in the distance. Putting her helmet back on, she looked in that direction and saw the vehicle Tank had been eyeing. She wished she could find the keys for that. Tank would love it. Immediately following that thought, she wondered why she cared, but she did. She'd hated the man, but the more time she spent around him, the more she found herself liking him.

There was still plenty of time. She might as well go look for the keys. She jumped out and walked back into the pavilion. Going to Bryce's body, she checked his pockets. Sure enough, in a pocket on his jacket was a set of keys. She went back outside and hit the unlock button. The lights flashed on the last vehicle in the line.

"Yes!"

That was easy. Going over to the Hummer, she jumped into the driver's seat and was about to start it, but something stopped her. It was night and everything was quiet. If she started this thing up, it would not only be loud but the lights would turn on. That left only one option. She'd have to carry everything. It actually worked out, because she wanted to be busy anyway. It took her fifteen minutes to haul everything from the back of the Hummer to the back of the Terradyne Gurkha LAPV. She then went into the supply pavilion and started grabbing all the food and water she could, filling the back of the LAPV. She set their backpacks on the seat in the third row. Having done that, she checked the Hummer one last time, and it was a good thing. She'd forgotten Tank's iPod and Bryce's journal. Back in the LAPV, she searched the glove box until she found the manual. With nothing better to do, she read through it.

It was built on the frame of a Ford F-550 Super Duty that was then outfitted with ballistic protection. It had military-grade tires, exterior and interior bullet-proofing armor, including the windows, blast-mitigating floor and seats, solid metal bumper with a winch on the front, and all the interior amenities of a top-of-the-line truck. Even though she understood little about how the engine was upgraded and the suspension was special, she did understand one thing—this vehicle was almost indestructible.

Returning the manual to the glove box, she locked the doors and leaned the seat back. She was exhausted from hauling all the gear. Some of the bags had weighed well over fifty pounds. The guys were going to love this thing, especially Tank. Things would probably get bloody when they fought amongst themselves about who was going to drive, but she had little doubt Tank would end up claiming the vehicle. And this time there was no way he could wreck it. Not that he did any of the other times, but she had to make sure to mention that. It'd piss him off. Thinking about Tank brought the memory of him hugging her to mind, and that thought made her smile as she dozed off.

19

THE CHASE

Post-outbreak day 8, early morning

Ana watched in her rearview mirror as the headlights continued to gain on her. She needed to do something, quick. Making it north of Sheridan on I-90 had been a miracle. She figured the truck would have died long before, but it was still going strong, minus the fact that smoke kept rising from the engine and obscuring her vision. Otherwise, things were going great. She was being chased by what seemed like all of the remaining Reclaimers, and her truck was going to stop running or explode any second, but even with all that, this was the most alive she'd felt in a long time. There was no one for her to protect, no one to worry about but herself. She hadn't realized how caged and stressed she'd been with the rest of the group, especially after they'd rescued all the people from Burns.

But now she was alone and it felt right. She should've left a long time ago. Her mind flashed back to Emmett, Alexis, and Jane rescuing her in the mall, and to all the time she and Alexis had spent in the backseat of the truck. They'd been a family, or the closest thing she had anymore. Her heart ached. She would miss them.

Oh stop it, she told herself. *I'm perfectly happy on my own.*

It would be much easier this way. There was still a part of her that regretted leaving them, but she'd never had any intention of meeting them at the border. Her priority was to lead the Reclaimers away. If she happened to live through the night, she'd deal with that later. For now she had to focus on killing them. Mainly Jezz. Because with her alive, Ana had no doubt that she would hunt them all to the end of the Earth to pay them back for what they'd done. That was just the type of crazy she was.

Glancing over, she took stock of her weapons. The AK-47 sat in the passenger seat, along with three full magazines, including the one in it. That was it. That's all she had. Well, that and an old tire iron lying on the floorboard in the back seat. She didn't think it'd be very effective trying to take on probably two dozen Reclaimers, but it was the only option she had. The farther she made it, the more likely it would be that Alexis and the rest would escape.

She continued to drive north. The interstate made a jog west for a bit but then straightened and turned north again. She passed a blue sign that read, "Welcome to Montana." Not that it mattered now, but she'd always wanted to come here. Now she could say she'd been to Montana, and all it'd taken was the end of civilization.

After almost an hour of driving, she decided it was time to make her move. The horizon was beginning to brighten and she was losing the cover of night. The Reclaimers had gained on her, but they were still far enough behind for her ambush to work.

Up ahead, there were a couple of crashed vehicles in her lane. If she added her truck to them, it'd stop the Reclaimers dead in their tracks. They could always go into the median to get around, of course, but it would slow them, at least. A line of trees sat east of the interstate and would be the perfect place for her to hide where they couldn't follow with vehicles. She'd get them on the defensive, then run for it and hopefully escape.

She turned the lights off and then the truck itself. It began to slow and she pulled the parking brake. The truck squealed and shuddered to a stop, lightly slamming into the two other vehicles, forming a makeshift barricade. She grabbed her rifle, magazines, and the tire iron. Running into the ditch to the east, she hopped the barbed wire fence and charged into the trees, then dropped to a knee behind the largest tree she could find. Shoving the tire iron into her belt behind her back and the magazines into her pockets, she readied herself. The AK-47 had a red-dot sight, which would be perfect for the hundred-or-so-yard shots. She rested the wooden handguard in a notch on the tree.

Just as she finished situating herself, the Reclaimers slowed by the barricade. She'd thought maybe she could just bail and they would continue on, but she'd scrapped that plan when she realized the smoking truck would be a dead giveaway. The line of six vehicles stopped completely and she aimed at the front one, waiting for the right moment. The man in the passenger's seat opened the door and stepped out, looking around. Before he'd fully settled on the ground, a 7.62x39mm bullet tore through his chest. He collapsed as the driver looked over, reaching for his gun. She fired again, the bullet tearing through the driver's shoulder.

By now the Reclaimers were starting to realize what was going on. Instead of going for the already wounded man, she aimed at the last vehicle in line. In the darkness, she couldn't see exactly where the window was, but she went off the placement of the headlights. Firing a few rounds at that spot, she switched to the third vehicle in line where a woman had gotten out. The woman aimed down at the trees where Ana was and got off two shots before Ana dropped her. Most of the Reclaimers were out of their vehicles and firing down at her now. Woodchips flew off the tree she had taken cover behind so she dropped to the ground. Crawling ten yards farther down the line of trees, she rose to a kneeling position and sighted on one of the men hiding behind a truck. She squeezed the trigger and then quickly squeezed it again, having missed her first shot. Blood sprayed in the air as the man's neck exploded. Instead of aiming, she let loose with some rapid fire on the middle vehicles. The rifle clicked and she ejected the spent magazine.

As soon as she stopped shooting, the Reclaimers honed in on her location and began to fire. Bullets whizzed by her head. One struck a tree next to her and sent shrapnel into the left side of her face. She fell to the ground. Her face stung and there was blood on her cheek. It was time for the part of her plan where she ran.

To stay low, she started rolling down a gradual slope away from the interstate. She began to pick up momentum as the angle of the slope increased and she gripped her rifle tighter. Suddenly, the ground was no longer beneath her and she fell two feet into water. She stood up, dizzy from rolling that far, and acquired her bearings. She'd fallen into a small creek. If she followed it, she would be going away from the interstate. In the distance, she could still hear the Reclaimers firing into the trees after her. Hopefully, it would be a few minutes before they dared follow.

She climbed up the other side of the bank and started running beside the creek as best she could in the darkness. Branches slapped her in the face and she stumbled a few times, falling back into the water. Each time she climbed to her feet and continued on her way. She ran with reckless abandon, knowing that with each step there was a risk of twisting her ankle—or worse. That didn't slow her down. The people following her would do far worse than that. After a quarter mile, she arrived at a spot where the small creek went through a culvert under a dirt road.

Climbing onto the road, she glanced around. There looked to be a large shape in the darkness to the left. If it was a house, it would be her best chance to find a new ride. She ran toward it, noticing the gunfire in the distance had stopped. They would be following her now and would find her soon. She slowed, reaching for a new magazine. There hadn't been time to reload earlier. Her hand found an empty back pocket; the magazine was gone. Feeling around, she realized she'd lost the tire iron as well. Frantically, she checked her front pocket and her last magazine was still there. Relieved, she shoved it into the rifle and racked the action. She also had her knife shoved into her boot for the infected, at least.

The shape in the darkness turned out to be a small house. A car and a truck with a horse trailer were parked out front. She thought about holing up in the house, but she dismissed it. With only one magazine left, there was no way she'd survive. She went over to the truck and tried the door. It was locked. She tried the car next. Opening the door she stopped, hearing something. Spinning quickly, she saw a groaning silhouette coming at her in the darkness. The knife was in her hand before she knew it and she took a step toward the infected. With one smooth motion, she plunged the blade into its eye and it collapsed to the ground.

Going back to the car, she looked inside. It was clear. Sitting down, she searched for the keys. Nothing on the dash, in the center console, or behind the visor. Next, she looked under the seat and in the glove box. Still nothing.

Where are the damn keys? she thought and then cursed herself.

The keys were dangling halfway out of the ignition! The car turned over twice before starting. She was reaching to close the door when a bullet punched through the headrest. Ducking down, she shifted it into gear and slammed her foot on the gas. More bullets peppered the back of the car and tore holes through the windshield. The driver's side window shattered, but the car sped down the dirt road away from the shooters. Bullets continued to fly through the air around her. The gunfire slowed as she took a small bend in the road. By some miracle, she'd made it without getting hit, and it seemed, for now, that nothing vital in the car had been damaged.

After about a mile, the driveway met a paved road. She took a left, heading southwest. They'd be expecting her to continue north—or so she hoped. She drove on, heading under the interstate. When she hit a four-way intersection, she stayed on the road, which took a short jog north and then continued west. She didn't have any idea where she was going, but her goal was to put as much distance between the Reclaimers and herself as she could. Hopefully, they hadn't seen her cross under the interstate. If they had, she'd just have to make sure her trail was chaotic. She wouldn't stick to the main roads or any one direction.

If she found a good location, she'd hide the car and hole up, find some food and maybe some guns, and then start out on her own. Maybe she would continue north and one day join the others, but she doubted that. More than likely, she'd find somewhere she could make a life for herself and set up there.

Or you could go back, kill Jezz, and take her place. Lead the Re-claimers, become the woman you were meant to be, purred the dark part in her. It would be easy to do. Once Jezz was dead, the Reclaimers would follow anyone strong enough. As long as they were allowed to kill, they'd be content to follow. All she would—

What the hell was she thinking? She quickly closed the lid on the box that held that part of her, but it wouldn't shut entirely.

"Control," she said out loud. "I need to stay in control."

She needed somewhere to lay low for a while. But first she had to make sure the Reclaimers weren't following her. The road turned south and she followed it. She didn't know where she was headed or if she'd even survive the day, but she continued on. The sun brightened the sky and the Bighorn Mountains loomed in the distance. Before her lay the open road, her destination unknown.

20

RED SKY

"What do you mean, she's missing?" Tank asked, dropping the folder he'd been holding.

"I mean the Hummer's still here, but she's gone and so is all our gear," James said.

"Are you saying she took it?" Tank asked, getting heated.

"No," James said. "I'm saying someone came and took all our gear and kidnapped Chloe."

Connor walked into the pavilion. "Everything's gone, even your iPod."

"Who the hell would take an iPod and not just take the whole Hummer?" Tank asked.

"That's a good point," James said. "I didn't think of that."

"This doesn't make any sense," Connor said.

"Are we sure she didn't hide it somewhere?" Tank asked.

"Where would she hide it?" James asked. "And, a better question: why?"

"I don't know!" Tank yelled. "We just need to find her."

"It's okay, bro," Connor said, walking over and laying a hand on his shoulder. "We will."

"They couldn't have gotten far," James said. "Let's get the Hummer and go find them."

James exited the pavilion with Tank and Connor following close behind. Why would someone take all their stuff and Chloe but leave the Hummer? Or did they take all the gear and Chloe got away to hide somewhere? When they arrived at the Hummer, James jumped in the driver's seat, looking around for the keys.

"Hey, man," James said. "Where'd you leave the keys?"

"With Chloe, of course," Tank said, walking up.

"Then they're gone," Connor said. "Whoever took Chloe took the keys."

"Maybe we should look around here," James said. "Chloe could've seen them coming and hid."

"Good idea!" Tank said, turning and heading into the nearest pavilion.

"I'll check around the perimeter," Connor said, running north.

I guess that leaves me with checking the other vehicles, James thought.

Jogging over to the nearest SUV, he crouched down, looking underneath. There was a dark stain on the ground. James flipped up his NVGs and turned on the light attached to his ACR. Blood. It had dried and was at least a few days old, but something had definitely happened. There was a reason Bryce had been the only one alive. Who were these people? They were equipped like the military and wore similar uniforms, but all they had on them were nametags, and those seemed like nicknames—nothing else, no insignia or rank. Turning off his light, he stood up and flipped down his NVGs.

He glanced inside the vehicle, but it was hard to see anything through the tinted windows. The door wouldn't open, it was locked, just like the rest. Walking around the SUV and looking in every window, he couldn't see anything inside. The next SUV looked the same, devoid of anything living. He was on his way to the—what was it again? An LPV or LAPC or something—when Connor called out.

"You guys are gonna want to see this!"

Tank immediately ran out of the second pavilion toward where Connor was perched on the berm, looking north. James ran after Tank, saying a quick prayer.

Let her be alive, Lord. Please, just let her be alive.

He passed the downed helicopter, arriving at the berm.

"Holy…" Tank said from the top.

James crested the berm. "What the hell?"

On the other side was a gravesite. There were thirteen newly dug graves with makeshift wooden tombstones. There were also six open graves, as if whoever had done this had been prepared for more.

"This is just plain weird," Tank said.

"This had to be—" James began.

"It's Bryce, definitely him," Tank said, cutting him off.

"No doubt," Connor said.

"This must've been what he meant when he said he was still missing people," James said.

"He was crazy," Tank said.

"Definitely," Connor said.

"This is honestly creepy," James said.

"This is like some weird horror film," Connor said.

"Yeah," James said. "Maybe we should just go back and look for Chloe."

"You guys lookin' for me?" said a female voice from right behind them.

James turned quickly, sighting down his ACR.

"Whoa, boys," she said. "I didn't mean to scare you."

Chloe stood a few feet away, wearing one of the helmets, and she had a handgun stuffed into her pocket.

"Where the hell did you come from?" Tank asked, lowering his weapon.

James flicked his safety back on. "Oh, don't worry about scaring us. I just think I need a new pair of pants."

"I was in the LAPV," Chloe said. "I may have fallen asleep."

"Fallen asleep?" Tank asked.

"In the what?" Connor asked.

"The big armored vehicle," Chloe said.

"Let me get this straight," James said. "You found the keys to the armored vehicle, took *all* our gear from the Hummer, and carried it over there?"

"Yep," Chloe said, "I also loaded more food and water. There's a lot more room in it."

"Woman," Tank said. "I think I might be in love with you."

Chloe looked stunned. It was easy to tell even with her helmet on and NVGs down.

"I'm jokin'," Tank said, seeing her reaction.

"I know that," Chloe said, recovering quickly. "You're Tank, after all."

"He *is* Tank," Connor said.

"Well, now that we have all that sorted out," James said, "we still have our friends to rescue."

"You weren't able to earlier?" Chloe asked.

"Long story," Connor said, walking back toward their new ride.

"We'll fill you in once we get goin'," James said, then added quickly. "Shotgun!"

"It's okay, bro. I was going to let you have it anyway. I'm gonna go check the downed Black Hawk real quick." Connor said and ran off to the crashed helicopter.

James watched him go. They'd completely forgotten to check that.

"You do realize you could've called 'driver,' and been able to drive the beasty," Tank said, smiling from ear-to-ear.

"Dammit," James said. "I just..."

"Assumed that the giant tank-thing was mine?" Tank asked.

"Well, yeah," James said.

"Good call," Tank said.

They arrived at the vehicle and James took a good look at it. It was huge and had three rows of seats. It looked almost like a Humvee crossed with a giant SUV and outfitted with even more armor. He swore it looked like the kickass armored vehicles the special ops people drove in all the movies. Walking around to the passenger's side, he climbed into the front seat and Chloe climbed into the seat behind him. She didn't need to ask where to sit so it made sense strategically; she'd already picked up on that. She hardly seemed like the same person James had met a couple of days ago.

Connor ran back from the Black Hawk.

"Nothing," he said, by the rear driver's side door.

"Bro..." James said, standing outside the passenger door.

"Yeah?" Connor asked. He had a look on his face that told James his brother already knew what he was thinking.

"I can't sit shotgun," James said, walking around the front of the LAPV.

Connor met him halfway. "It's okay, bro."

James climbed into the seat behind Tank.

"What the hell was that about?" Tank said. "You don't feel honored enough to sit next to me? Do I smell?"

"You know exactly why," James said.

"Of course," Tank said. "It's not practical."

"Exactly," James said.

"For once, I agree with my brother," Connor said, shutting his door.

"Oh, I do too," Tank said, starting the LAPV. "But I'm still goin' to give him crap about it."

The engine roared to life, growling like a large beast. Tank turned it around and faced the road leading down the hill.

"Oh, yeah," Tank said. "This thing is a diesel and everything. I bet it has some serious power!" He gunned it and the vehicle lurched forward, shoving them into their seats.

"Someone wanna tell me what that was all about?" Chloe asked. "I'm in the correct seat, right?"

"Yes, you are," James said. "Connor is left-handed. He can shoot more easily from the passenger's side, and I can shoot better from the driver's side."

"Oh," Chloe said. "You guys put a lot of thought into this."

"Yeah, but a lot of it comes naturally," James said.

"So you've had some kind of training?" Chloe asked.

"Just Connor," James said, "but he was only in the corps for a year. Tank and I have nothing but what he taught us."

"What happened?" Chloe asked.

"I broke my leg," Connor said. "They medically discharged me."

"They forced you to leave?" Chloe asked. "Why?"

"They were downsizing the military, looking for any reason to kick us out. I just wanted to stay and heal, continue to do the only job I've ever wanted—defending our great nation—but I guess someone had other plans for me."

"Do you miss it?" Chloe asked.

"Before all this? Every day. Now, I'm glad I was here to stand with my brothers at the end."

"I'm glad you're here too, bro," James said.

"Me too," Tank said, pretending to wipe a tear from his eye.

James chuckled. "You're a piece of work, you know that?"

"Always have been," Tank said, "always will be."

They arrived at the intersection of US-14. The sun was beginning to brighten the sky. In thirty minutes, it'd be light enough to see, and in another hour the sun would be up.

"North?" Tank asked.

"Yeah," James said. "I don't see why they'd wanna go south."

"On it," Tank said.

Connor opened the glove box. "Look at this," he said, presenting the manual to James. "Will you do the honors?"

"Me?" James asked, taking the offered manual. "Hell yeah!"

"I read that already," Chloe said.

"And?" Tank asked.

"It's built on a Ford truck and is bulletproof," Chloe said.

"And?" Tank asked again.

"Some other vehicle stuff," Chloe said, shrugging. "I'm sure one of you will be able to understand it better than me."

James started scanning through it. With every page he read, he became more and more impressed with this vehicle. After five minutes, he had all the main components read.

"You guys aren't going to believe how badass this thing is!" James said.

"Oh, I do," Tank said. "I'm drivin' it!"

"Well, let me tell you," James said. "First, LAPV stands for Light Armored Patrol Vehicle. It has two layers of armor that can withstand 7.62mm armor-piercing rounds, has over four hundred horsepower, eight hundred and sixty pounds of torque, blast-resistant floor, a max speed of seventy miles-per-hour, a solid metal bumper, and upgraded shocks, axles, chassis, etc. It weighs sixteen hundred pounds, can drive through three feet of water, can—"

"We get it," Connor said.

"So this baby is damn near indestructible?" Tank asked, his smile growing as James talked.

"For everyone else," Chloe said. "I don't know about you with your track record."

James and Connor burst out laughing, while Tank just glared at her in the rearview mirror.

She shrugged. "Payback for the whole 'Arthas' thing."

Tank smirked despite himself. "Fair enough."

"Oh, man," James said, still chuckling. "She got you good."

"Shut up, Jamesy Boy," Tank said.

"Oh," Chloe said suddenly, "and I found this." She pulled out a thin leather book.

"What's that?" James asked.

"Bryce's journal," Chloe said. "I know who Elliot was."

"Really? Who?" James asked.

"His twelve-year-old son who died last year. Bryce has been hearing his voice and started talking to him a few months after his death. By June, he was acting like his son had never died. And," she said, pausing, "he was going to kill you guys today."

"What was he gonna do with you?" Tank asked.

"Try and marry me, I think," Chloe said, looking sick.

Tank started laughing. "Of course he was. I told you, you laid the flirting on a little too thick."

"Whatever," Chloe said.

"Wait, who cares about any of that," Connor said. "What does it say about the outbreak and what his people were doing there?"

"I never thought to check that," Chloe said.

"Typical woman," Tank said.

"At least I don't go around measuring my manhood with every other guy I meet," Chloe said.

"Gross," Tank said.

"Okay…" James said. "We need to check it out then."

"We might want to wait on that," Connor said.

They'd arrived at I-90 and Tank took them onto the ramp heading north toward Sheridan.

"We'd better keep our eyes open," James said. "No tellin' where they might be."

"Grab more magazines," Connor said to James, "and one of the ACRs with the longer barrel and a scope."

"On it," James said. "Oh, and guys, you didn't let me finish earlier. This thing has a latch on the roof where you can stand up and shoot."

"Damn," Tank said. "I'm definitely in love."

James climbed into the third seat and grabbed one of the black bags. Chloe had done a really good job of packing everything and the gear was easily accessible. He pulled out the longer-barreled DMR and handed it to his brother. Connor stuck his shorter ACR by the seat and racked a round into his new rifle. James grabbed one of the full ammunition cans with magazines and then one of the boxes with the only two other drum magazines for the SAW. Then he retrieved two of the Kel-Tec KSG tactical 12-gauge pump-action shotguns, setting them on the seat next to him. It was hard to believe that a weapon just over two feet long could hold fifteen shotgun shells.

"Switch me," Connor said.

"So you can get at the hatch?" James asked, grabbing one of the Kel-Tec shotguns and switching seats with his brother.

"Yeah, it'll give me a little height advantage," Connor said.

"Fine by me," James said from the passenger's seat. "Just watch yourself up there."

"I will," Connor said.

They suddenly grew quiet. There was no telling what waited for them up ahead. The Reclaimers could have recaptured or killed their friends, or they could be waiting for them, knowing they were coming. They continued north of Sheridan, the sun painting the cloudy sky crimson.

"That's a beautiful sunrise," Chloe said.

"Don't you get them like this all the time up here?" Tank asked.

"Yeah, they call it 'big sky country' for a reason," James said.

"Red sky in the morning," Connor said, "sailors take warning. There's a storm comin'."

21

NO MATTER THE COST

T he infected's head exploded, its mouth a mere inch from biting into his leg, and Emmett wasted no time shooting the next infected. Rising to his knees, he took aim and shot another. Once on his feet, he turned and rushed back to the truck. He jumped in, started the engine, and spun the truck around, leaving the house and infected behind.

"Why were there so many of them in there?" Troy asked.

"No idea," Lucas said, "but that was close."

Emmett looked at Greg and nodded. "Thanks."

"Don't mention it," Greg said.

"Why were they all inside?" Troy asked. "It's almost like they were hiding or something."

"Maybe they were staying out of the wind or sunlight," Lucas said.

"I hope not," Emmett said. "If so, they're more intelligent than we think."

"Now what?" Troy asked.

"There was something farther up the road," Lucas said.

"We'll check it out," Emmett said, turning onto the highway and heading north.

"See," Lucas said, pointing.

"Looks like some kind of staging area for the mine," Greg said.

"Would you look at that?" Troy said. "I see one, two vehicles parked out front."

"That'll work," Emmett said, pulling next to the white truck and van.

He stopped the truck, leaving it running, and got out. Glancing around, he didn't see any infected.

"Make it quick," Emmett said.

Lucas ran over to the van and opened the door, getting in. After searching around for a bit, he climbed back out. "Nothing," he said. "No keys."

"I could hot-wire them," Greg said, stepping from the truck.

"That won't help us in the long run," Emmett said. "Greg, you and I will head inside the office and look for the keys. You two stay out here and keep watch."

"Got it," Lucas said.

Emmett walked toward the small building the vehicles were parked in front of. Could they be so lucky as to find the keys inside? Judging by the blue-and-black logo on the side of the vehicles, they were company-owned. With luck, that meant they kept the keys on site. He approached the door and nodded to Greg.

"What?" Greg asked.

Oh, right, Emmett thought. *He doesn't have any training.*

"When I nod, open the door," Emmett said. "I'll go in first, then you follow. I'll go left, you go right."

"Easy enough," Greg said.

"And pay attention. No telling what's inside," Emmett said.

He nodded again. This time Greg did his part and Emmett peered into the room before going in. With the infected, he had to adjust his normal training. These things weren't like armed tangos. They behaved a lot differently. Inside was clear, with only one door leading to a small bathroom. It was clear also.

"Check for the keys," Emmett said, looking around the room.

On the left side was a small kitchenette with a couple of couches along the back wall next to it. To the right sat a counter with a computer behind it, and the back corner held the bathroom. Greg was already behind the counter, searching. Emmett turned and looked by the door. There was an empty coat hanger, a small table with an empty bowl, and what looked like a key hook. It was also empty.

"Got 'em," Greg said, holding up two sets of keys.

Greg walked out from behind the counter and out the door to the vehicles. Emmett followed, closing the door to the office. Greg tossed the set for the van to Lucas and walked over to the truck.

"Nice," Lucas said, walking to the van with Troy following.

"Make sure they start and have enough gas," Emmett said.

Both vehicles started.

"Mine's good," Greg said.

"I have a quarter of a tank," Lucas said. "So good enough for now."

"Roll out and meet back at the other rigs," Emmett said.

He climbed into his truck and led the way to where they'd left the rest of their group. Arriving a minute later, Emmett was happy to see nothing had changed while they'd been gone. He half imagined he'd come back and see nothing but the burning wreckage of what was left of his life.

"I told you I'd see you soon," Alexis said as he climbed out.

"Yes, you did," Emmett said, then turned to the rest of them. "Everyone ready?"

"I think so," Helen said.

"Good. Find a vehicle and let's hit the road," Emmett said.

"And don't be afraid to spread out," Alexis said. "We have plenty of room now."

Olive and Felix climbed into the backseat of Emmett's truck.

"Hello, Mr. Emmett," Olive said.

"Hey, Olive," he said.

Alexis watched as all the kids and adults loaded into the four other vehicles. Then she climbed into the passenger's seat of the truck. Emmett pulled his truck parallel with the other vehicles.

"I'll lead," Emmett said. "Greg, bring up the rear and let's keep our eyes open. If we can make good time, we'll be at the border before nightfall."

"Which way are you going?" Troy asked from the driver's seat of the truck they'd taken from the Reclaimers.

"I was told you knew a good way to stay off the interstate," Emmett said.

"I do," Troy said. "We'll want to stay on MT-314 'till we get to US-212. Take that up to MT-39. We'll stay on there until it runs into I-94."

"Good," Emmett said. "You can tell me the rest after we stop and pick up a map. Stay within sight and keep track of the vehicle following you. If anyone gets into trouble, flash your hazard lights."

"Sounds good," Lucas said from the driver's seat of the minivan.

"Move out," Emmett said, driving past the line of vehicles.

The other rigs turned around and fell in line behind him. Arriving at MT-314, he turned north. The rest followed and they topped out at a good cruising speed. The sparsely furnished hills rolled out all around them. This part of the country was pretty bleak, with nothing but small trees and sagebrush. Emmett liked that—a lot of open country and not a lot of people. If they hadn't had the fallback house in Alaska or didn't think they could reasonably make it, he would set up in this country on a hill where he could see for a good long way.

"Felix," Alexis said, "how'd you get a black eye?"

"That is a pretty good shiner," Emmett said.

Red rose in his cheeks. "The guys back there were picking on the kids so I attacked them. It didn't do much good."

"That's a lie," Olive said. "They were picking on me and Felix punched one in the face. Gave him a bloody lip. Then they hit him."

"Are you okay?" Alexis asked.

"Yeah, I'm fine," Felix said. "Just a little sore."

"That was very brave," Emmett said.

"Thanks," Felix said, then grew quiet. After a minute he spoke up. "Mr. Wolfe?"

"Just call me Emmett," he said.

"Emmett," Felix said, "can you teach me to shoot?"

"Of course, kid," Emmett said.

"I told you," Alexis said, smiling back at him.

"I just wasn't sure," Felix said.

"Why?" Emmett asked.

"Well, I'm only ten," Felix said.

"That doesn't matter anymore," Emmett said. "You're going to have to step up and be a man now. I'll teach you to shoot. But I won't let you have a gun until I know you understand when it should be used and what the consequences are."

"That's okay with me," Felix said, excitement in his voice.

"Good," Emmett said. "Next time we stop I'll show you how to properly hold a rifle and the rules you need to follow. Then, when we have somewhere safe to practice, you can shoot."

"Sweet!" Felix said.

"Can you teach me, too?" Olive said.

"Sure," Emmett said. Alexis looked over at him disapprovingly. "But you can't shoot one of these rifles just yet. You can watch while I teach Felix. Everyone should know gun safety, whether you're shooting yet or not."

"Yes!" Olive said, looking triumphant.

"You sure that's a good idea?" Alexis whispered to him. "She's only eight."

"I was six when my father taught me to shoot," Emmett said. "Plus it's the end of the world. They need to know how to protect themselves."

"You know we can hear you," Olive said.

"I'm just worried about you," Alexis said, looking back at her.

"I know," Olive said, "but I've had to take care of myself for a while now."

"You still amaze me," Alexis said. "You know that?"

"Yeah, I'm kinda awesome," Olive said.

"Oh, really?" Emmett said. "Don't go gettin' a big head now."

"Big head?" Olive asked.

"Yeah, like prideful or cocky," Emmett said.

"Oh," Olive said, giggling. "That's a funny way to say it."

"A little before your time, maybe," Emmett said.

"Before all of our times," Alexis said.

"I'm not *that* old," Emmett said.

"You could be my grandpa," Olive said.

"Hey!" Emmett said.

Alexis started laughing, and Felix and Olive joined in.

"Grandpa Emmett," Olive said.

The laughter died down after awhile.

"It feels good to laugh," Alexis said.

"My mom always used to say laughter is the best medicine," Olive said. "Whenever we were at the hospital, she'd always make me laugh. It would help with the pain."

"Your mom was a wise woman," Alexis said.

Olive nodded, sniffling. "Do you think James will find us?"

"If anyone can do it, James and Connor can," Alexis said.

"Don't worry about them," Emmett said. "They'll meet up with us at the border."

"Good. I miss him," Olive said.

"Me too," Alexis said.

Emmett glanced at his daughter. She was gazing out the window, twirling a piece of loose hair between her fingers. The look on her face and her fidgeting spoke volumes. She was worried about James and Connor. They fell into silence as the miles slipped by and the sun climbed higher behind the clouds, which blocked it from view. It was going to rain today, if the clouds were any indication. It didn't look overly threatening, just a light shower.

Emmett thought back to the incident by the house that morning. That had been a little too close. He hadn't worried about it in the moment, but now that he had a little time to think, the outcome played in his mind. If Greg hadn't stepped up, he might not have been quick enough to stop that infected from taking a chunk out of his leg. Then he'd end up like Jane—his wife. He hadn't thought about her since she'd died. Even though they hadn't been on good terms for the last few years, he still had feelings for her. She'd been his only wife, and after the divorce he'd never considered remarrying. Mason's death had been the straw that broke the camel's back, but he didn't hate Jane for it. In fact, he didn't blame her at all. He blamed himself.

Nothing had been the same after that. Jane had grown even more distant, and Emmett dove headfirst into his deployment, trying to fight the feelings of guilt. Less than a year later, they were separated and Jane had Alexis. At the time, he didn't think he could raise a daughter so he hadn't fought the custody hearing—in fact, he was overseas. But after another year, he realized that if he couldn't be there for his son, he had to be around to see his daughter grow up. He'd finished his tour and left the corps three years later. It was the easiest and hardest decision he ever made. To this day, he carried the guilt of leaving his brothers behind. But his daughter needed a father, and he was going to be there.

It'd been the joy of his life to watch his daughter grow into the woman she was, and he'd do anything he could to keep her alive and be there for her. That'd almost changed today from one little slip. The world had become just like the battlefield—one small mistake and it could cost him and those around him their lives. There would come a time when he wouldn't be around anymore. But until that day, he would keep a sharp eye out. A careless mistake like the one earlier couldn't be allowed to happen again, and he would make sure it didn't.

"Ana's not going to meet up with us," Alexis said, drawing Emmett from his contemplations.

Both of the kids were asleep in the backseat. They'd had a long couple of days. He was surprised they were able to keep going as well as they were.

"What do you mean?" Emmett asked.

"I mean, she's going her own way."

"She said she was going to join up with us."

"Her eyes said something different. She's not coming back."

"What happened?"

"She killed them dad. Mila and Evan. I can still see it."

A tear slipped from her eye.

"I'm sorry, sweetie. I know that's hard to handle. Did she explain why she did it?"

"She said she did it for me, but I can't accept that. I don't want this on me."

More tears started to streak down her cheeks.

"It's not on you. It's on her. She may have had good motives and done it to rescue the group, or it might have been to save herself. Either way, it was her choice and she's the one who has to live with it. Not you."

"I just thought I knew her better than that. The woman who killed Evan, whatever her motives, wasn't the same Ana I knew."

"She's had a hard life. I can only imagine what her childhood was like. She made the choice she felt was best, and Alexis, I support it." His daughter looked at him, scrunching up her brow. The vulnerability in her eyes broke his heart. "I do. It enabled her to rescue you. Even if I hadn't shown up, she would've been able to get you out. That's what matters most to me—your safety. I would kill anyone to save your life, no matter the cost."

"Please don't ever kill an innocent person for me."

"I can't promise you that. I'll do whatever it takes to keep you safe. But don't worry. The only killing we should have to do is the infected and evil people."

"But how do you know the bad ones from the good? How can you make that call?"

"Thoughtfully, but in the end you usually only have a split second, and you have to trust your instincts. I was trained extensively to tell the bad guys from the good. When someone is shooting at you, it's always easier. It's harder when they haven't threatened you yet. It's never easy to take a life, but it *is* necessary sometimes."

His daughter wiped the tears from her face and stared out the window. What Emmett told her was the truth, but it wasn't that cut and dry. There were some who were pure evil and enjoyed killing. Others, like himself, were willing to kill to protect what they had, and others were just desperate. In the end, anyone who threatened his life and the life of those he cared about was a "bad guy," and he'd end them. There would be no hesitation, no thinking. He would give them a swift death so his daughter could live. *Was* that right? Probably not, but it was what he would do.

The world had come to a place where he had two choices—survive or die. He would survive as long as he could, ensuring Alexis's safety. She had her whole life ahead of her, if they could just live long enough to get to Alaska. Then, she could have a new life, and he prayed they could make it before the world took more from them.

22

GUNS BLAZING

*W*e're ready for this, Connor thought. *We have to be.*

He sat in the middle of the backseat, ready to open the hatch in the roof. Chloe had moved to the third row of seats, so now he could get out from either side. They were back in Montana, having just crossed the state boundary. This was where their journey had begun. It'd been another hundred and fifty miles to the northeast, but they'd almost made a full circle. It felt weird.

So far, it'd been quiet since Sheridan, with no sign of their group or the Reclaimers. A few zombies roamed around here and there, but nothing to worry about. The sun was hidden behind the nimbostratus clouds, and he knew it would rain today. There were five-hundred-foot ceilings and only a half-mile visibility. This wouldn't be a good day for flying, that was for sure. He thought about Alaska and couldn't wait to soar through the sky again—the trees and lakes passing below, the mountains rising beside the small plane, and the freedom that only came with flying.

I-90 took a shallow curve to the left and they began to descend into the barren hill country south of Wyola. They drove through a small pass, hills rising on both sides. Being higher than the country before them, he could see for miles and miles. Below them, the interstate continued north, taking a shallow curve back to the right and disappearing behind a hill. Something caught Connor's eye. At the base of the hill sat a few vehicles, and there were people around those vehicles.

"Damn!" Tank said, slamming on the brakes and swerving off the road to the right.

The vehicles had been just at the edge of sight, and once the angle changed as they dropped into the ditch, they vanished.

"What?" James asked, sitting up straight.

"There are people in front of us," Connor said.

"Reclaimers?" James asked, coming fully awake.

"I think so," Connor said.

"It looked like 'em," Tank said. "What's the plan?"

Connor looked around. The hill the people were behind could be climbed from this side without them seeing. At the top there were pockets of green brush and a few tan-colored sandstone outcroppings. It would be perfect cover and only about a three-hundred-yard shot. His Bushmaster ACR DMR, with its turret-adjusting scope would make the shots easier.

"Drop me off here and let me get to the top of the hill," Connor said. "I'll confirm they're Reclaimers, then start picking them off once you guys go in and keep them distracted."

"So shock 'n awe," James asked, "with you on overwatch?"

"Roger," Connor said.

"Hell, yeah," Tank said. "We'll go in with guns blazin'!"

"Keep 'em off my back," Connor said, grabbing his AR and slinging it over his shoulder, just in case.

"We will. You sure you wanna go out there alone?" James asked.

"Yeah, it's far enough that they'll have a hard time hitting me, unless they take the time to really aim, and it's up to you guys to prevent that," Connor said, opening the back door and stepping out.

"Oh, I can cause some mayhem," Tank said, that mischievous glint in his eye.

"Good luck," James said. "You mess with the best..."

"You die like the rest," Connor said, before he turned and started up the hill.

"Tank, I need to borrow your SAW," James said, climbing into the back seat.

"But I never got first blood," Tank said.

Chloe rolled her eyes.

"I know, but I need it," James said, setting his ACR down on the seat beside him.

"You always have to ruin the fun," Tank said. "Just like my 'stang."

"That was a safety issue," James said. "We had to make it—"

"Practical," Tank said. "Yeah, I know. It's already in the back. Just make sure the first time is memorable."

"Don't worry, I will," James said.

"You're so weird," Chloe said from the back.

"You might wanna buckle up," Tank said. "It's about to get bumpy."

"I am," Chloe said. "Just don't wreck us."

James chuckled as he picked up the SAW.

"You need me to do anything?" Chloe asked.

"Just stay buckled and keep your head down," James said.

"I can do that," Chloe said.

"That dude is fast," Tank said, watching Connor hike up the hill.

"He'll need a little time at the top to get situated," James said.

"I figured," Tank said, checking over his plate carrier and tightening his helmet.

"It's going to get *that* bumpy?" Chloe asked.

"It might," Tank said.

"Don't go too crazy at first," James said. "I'll need enough time to get some rounds down range. We need to draw their attention first, then Connor will open fire. With the chaos and the suppresser masking his shots, he'll be harder to locate. Best case, they won't even know he's there."

"Just like a damn ghost," Tank said.

"Exactly," James said. "He's at the top."

"I see that," Tank said. "How long you wanna give him?"

"A couple minutes," James said.

"Isn't this waiting killing you?" Chloe said after a minute of silence. "I'm freakin' out back here."

"Oh yeah," Tank said. "I'm just good at holdin' it inside."

"Same," James said.

"At least I'm not the only one," Chloe said. "What about Connor?"

"Prolly not," James said at the same time Tank said, "Nope."

"He's stalkin' his prey right now," James said.

"I almost feel sorry for 'em," Tank said.

"They deserve what they got comin'," James said.

"Oh, I agree," Tank said. "I just hope Connor saves some for us."

After a couple of minutes, James glanced up at the hilltop. Connor should've had enough time to set up by now.

"Ready?" James asked.

"Almost," Tank said, scrolling through his iPod. "Got it!"

Comin' in Hot by Hollywood Undead began to play as Tank stepped on the gas and they swerved back onto the interstate.

Connor crawled to the peak of the hill and lay next to a sandstone mound. It would obscure most of his body and be a good place to take cover if he needed it. He'd been mistaken about one thing, though. It was at least four hundred yards, maybe a little over. His first shot would be a good indication of how far it really was. The biggest gamble was assuming that the ACR he had was zeroed and would actually hit where it should. At this distance, there was little room for error. Dialing the scope to four hundred yards and turning it all the way to twenty-four power, he looked through it and then slowly backed off the power to sixteen to get the best field of view and less shake. His

AR lay next to him, ready to rock and roll. Then, he waited. Tank and James would be heading in soon.

He watched the men and women. Connor couldn't confirm for sure that they were Reclaimers. They weren't wearing anything special—like Xs painted in blood on their chests. They did have some heavy firepower and even an RPG. That would be the one he took down first. More than likely they were the Reclaimers, but he'd have to wait and see.

There were ten of them and five vehicles. Well, five working vehicles. There were three more that made what looked like a blockade—a truck was even smoking. It seemed like the other five might've taken fire and there was one missing. When the Reclaimers pulled out of their hideout, they'd had six vehicles. Where was the silver SUV that the black-haired woman had climbed into? Two more men and a woman walked out of the trees to the east. That made thirteen total. Not as many as he would've guessed, there were definitely some missing. As he watched, the three newcomers walked up to a man who seemed to be in charge. Connor would take him down second.

A vehicle revved up back to his left, and quickly glancing around, he confirmed it was Tank. It was go time. James was peeking out of the hatch on top with the SAW, bipod down on the roof. They rounded the slight corner and were in plain sight of the men and women down below, who began to fire on them without hesitation. James let loose with the SAW. Whether they were Reclaimers or not, at this point they were hostiles and that was all Connor needed to know.

The woman with the RPG moved to take a knee. Crosshairs settling on her chest, Connor slowly released his breath and squeezed the trigger. The round tore through her leg as she knelt. He quickly dialed the turret on his scope to four hundred and fifty yards. Crosshairs settling on her again, he noticed one of the men had scooped up the RPG. Connor readjusted and fired. The bullet slammed into his chest and he collapsed, firing the RPG as he fell. It hit one of their trucks and exploded. Two men went down with the blast, and it knocked more off their feet. The man who was presumably the leader took cover behind the makeshift blockade. As he fired on the LAPV, a bullet whizzed by his head from James. He ducked back down. Connor had a shot through a window in one of the vehicles, and he squeezed the trigger, but the bullet punched into the door just to the right of the window.

Connor cursed, steadied himself, and fired again. This time the bullet shattered the window and entered the leader's head. He collapsed. Acquiring a new target, Connor watched as another fell to James's fully automatic fire. One of the women shot an AK-47 at the LAPV as it sped towards them. Connor aimed at her and fired, hitting her in the shoulder. She staggered back and was raising her rifle again when another bullet center-punched her. Connor found a man lying prone next to a truck, firing on the LAPV, and he sent a bullet through that man's chest and into the pavement.

Something slammed into the rock next to Connor's face, sending out a small explosion of dust and debris. They were firing at him. Another slammed into the ground in front of him. Searching, he found the man lying partway in a ditch with a bolt-action rifle. A bullet streaked by Connor's head, and he returned fire but missed his mark by an inch. The man didn't even flinch. He fired again and the bullet ricocheted off of Connor's helmet. He cursed, rolling behind the rock.

Comin' in Hot by Hollywood Undead blared through the speakers as they rounded the corner. The people saw them and immediately started firing.

"They're shooting at us!" James yelled from the roof of the vehicle.

"Then shoot back!" Tank yelled as he sped up.

James aimed at the largest group of them and opened fire. To say he was aiming would be a lie. He was throwing as much ammunition as he could at them from the top of a moving vehicle, so he was surprised when two of them dropped to the ground in a spray of blood. He continued to let them have it as they began to dive for cover. Two were behind a truck and James fired on them. After a few rounds, the truck exploded.

"Holy..." James said.

Bullets ricocheted off the LAPV and James lowered his profile in the hatch as he continued to fire, trying to focus more on aiming where the Reclaimers were clustered behind the vehicles. A man stepped from behind the front end of a truck and James filled him full of lead. He fell to the ground, having taken three rounds. They were only two hundred yards out now and closing fast. James continued to fire, surprised the gun hadn't run out of ammunition yet. Two hundred rounds was a lot compared to a thirty. He dropped a woman who tried running into the trees right before his ammunition ran out. A bullet smacked into the hatch door beside his head, and he quickly ducked back inside.

Surprisingly, only two rounds had hit the windshield, both on the passenger's side. He grabbed his ACR and popped his head back out. Two of the hostiles jumped into the middle truck and started to pull out. They had to maneuver their way out before they were free of the other vehicles. A man stood up in the ditch and began to run toward the trees. James shot four rounds at him, but all of them missed, and he disappeared into the trees. James shot a few more rounds into the trees to encourage the man on his way. Tank began to slow the vehicle down. They were only fifty yards away from the truck. Moving his sights to the truck trying to get away, he aimed at the driver's-side window and opened fire. Bullets shattered the glass and the driver slumped against the wheel. The passenger jumped out with his hands in the air.

"Don't—" he was cut off as a bullet slammed into his neck.

Connor.

Tank slowed the LAPV to a crawl and James glanced around at the vehicles and bodies on the ground. Blood covered the pavement and vehicles, and pooled under bodies. They were all dead.

"I think we got 'em," James yelled down at Tank.

"Hell yeah, we did!" Tank said as James came back inside. "I just wish I could've joined in. I didn't even get to run anyone over."

James chuckled as he switched out his partial magazine for a full one.

"Did you see me blow that truck up?" James asked, still yelling from the ringing in his ears.

"Yeah," Tank said. "I didn't think that'd happen in real life."

"Me either," James said. "Let's clear the area, just watch the trees where the one got away."

"Of course," Tank said.

"Let me know when it's safe to come out," Chloe said.

"Gotcha," Tank said, opening his door.

"Chloe," James asked. "Could you hand me one of the drum magazines for the SAW."

"Sure," she said as she grabbed one from a bag on the seat, handing it to him.

"Thanks," James said, taking it and stepping out.

He could see Connor coming down the hill over four hundred yards away. He grabbed the SAW and drum magazine and spent a minute reloading it. Tank walked over to his side and watched as James struggled to get it reloaded. Once done, he handed it to Tank.

"Put a hundred rounds into the trees over there," James said pointing at the tree line. "Make sure our friend is long gone."

"Don't mind if I do," Tank said, walking over to a truck.

Resting the bipod on the hood, he opened fire and bullets peppered the foliage, slamming into wood and cutting through leaves. He did it in bursts, taking a break every few shots and then starting to shoot at a different location. If the last survivor was smart, he would make for the hills.

As Tank covered the trees, James walked up to the first body, drawing his tomahawk. He slammed it into the man's skull. Moving on to the next, he repeated the process. They needed to be sure none of them would come back. He pulled the blade of the tomahawk from the sixth body, a man who'd been burned to a crisp in the explosion. A noise came from his left on the other side of an SUV.

"I got an undead over here," Tank said, as his suppressive fire stopped.

"One of the people we just killed?" James asked, astonished.

"Yep," Tank said. "Hasn't been dead for more than a couple minutes."

"Why so soon?" James said. "It usually takes longer."

"Must've been bitten at some point," Tank said, shooting it in the head with his SAW. "There, at least I got to kill something."

James chuckled, turning around to finish his work. His brother was only a hundred yards out now, but movement caught his attention on the ground ten yards away. It was a woman with a handgun aimed at him. He didn't even have time to raise his rifle as a bullet slammed into his chest.

23

LAME DEER

Post-outbreak day 8, late morning

E mmett took in the town of Lame Deer, but there wasn't much left to see. It seemed that the apocalypse had been brutal there. Trash was scattered everywhere and all of the houses looked rundown and ransacked. Someone had come through this town with a vengeance, which was odd since it was literally in the middle of nowhere. He pulled to a stop at the intersection of US-214 and MT-39 when Troy flashed his hazard lights, pulling up next to Emmett's truck.

"I hate to stop in Lame Deer," Troy said, "but I'm dangerously low on gas and I don't think I'll make it to Colstrip."

"Okay," Emmett said, looking around at the few infected shambling toward their vehicles.

"Take a right here," Troy said. "I think I remember the gas station being down a block or so."

They turned down the street, Emmett counting the infected they passed. By the time they arrived at the gas station he'd counted two dozen. There were another three in the parking lot. He pulled to a stop next to one of the pumps.

"Watch my back," Emmett said.

Alexis nodded as he grabbed his machete and stepped out. She stepped out after him, aiming her handgun as he took down the first one. He moved on to the next, and before the last vehicle had pulled in, he had all three on the ground.

"Fill up quickly!" Emmett said. "We have at least two dozen infected heading our way. If you need to piss, hold it. We can stop in a more secure location."

"This place was hit hard," Alexis said.

"No, this is how Lame Deer always looks," Troy said. "There's a reason they call it Lame Deer."

"Oh," Alexis said.

"What should we do about food?" Helen asked through the passenger window of the minivan.

"This may be our best chance to forage," Lucas said.

"Okay," Emmett said. "Greg, Lucas, Alexis you're with me."

"I think I'd be better here," Alexis said, "for when the infected show up."

Emmett eyed her. He really didn't want to let her out of his sight, although it may be safer out there than inside the gas station.

He sighed. "Just be careful. You two ready?"

"Yeah," Lucas said. He had the Glock handgun tucked into his pants behind his back and held a large wrench.

Greg nodded. He was armed with the ACR and had a hammer tucked into his belt.

"I'll go first," Emmett said, brandishing his machete. "Let's keep it quiet. Lucas, you follow, and Greg, keep the rifle handy in case it gets intense."

They walked up to the front door of the gas station and Emmett banged on it. He waited a few seconds, then opened the door. Two infected stumbled out. He and Lucas made quick work of them. Emmett led the way inside, pulling out his flashlight. Scanning, he saw that most of the contents of the shelves had been taken. There were a few items scattered around the floor, though. He grabbed a grocery bag from behind the counter and handed one to Lucas.

"Grab all you can," Emmett said, picking up a candy bar off the floor.

It only took them a minute to collect everything, and it was a measly find—only two grocery bags half full of junk food and a couple of sodas. They exited the gas station and he noticed immediately that there were six new corpses on the ground. Alexis was a little ways from the vehicle with two infected coming at her. Emmett drew his Beretta and aimed at the closest one, but stayed his hand. One day he wouldn't be around and she needed to be able to handle herself. He watched as she took down the first one with a piece of rebar, stabbing it through the eye. Then she pulled her knife. He shuddered. That would put her dangerously close to the infected. Again he waited as she plunged her knife into the infected's eye and it dropped to the ground, tearing the knife from her grip as it fell. She quickly bent down and jerked the blade from its skull, then wiped it off on the infected's shirt.

"She's quite a woman, isn't she?" Troy said as Emmett walked over to his truck.

Emmett grunted, narrowing his eyes at Troy, who didn't notice because he was watching Alexis. She walked back over, and Troy went back to the truck he was driving.

"Everyone filled up?" she asked. They all confirmed. "Well, what're we waiting for? We're burnin' daylight!"

She climbed into the passenger's seat and smiled sweetly at Emmett. She was telling him she could handle herself, which he knew but tended to forget sometimes. He just wanted to protect her. Was being overprotective that bad, he wondered. He guessed it probably was.

"Hey," Troy said, coming back over.

"What do you want?" Emmett asked, climbing into the driver's seat. Everyone else was in their vehicles and ready to go.

"You mind if I ride with you?" he said, glancing over at Alexis.

"Not a chance," Emmett said.

"But—" Troy began, his smile fading.

"Get your ass back to your truck, now," Emmett said, and his tone left no room for negotiation.

"What was that about?" Alexis asked as Troy left.

"Nothing," Emmett said.

"You said a bad word," Olive said.

"Yes, I did," Emmett said. "Sometimes it's necessary to get your point across."

"So I can say it if I need to?" Olive said.

"No, you have to be at least twelve," Emmett said.

"What?" Alexis said. "They shouldn't even be saying that at twelve."

"It's just a donkey," Felix said.

"Yeah, like a jackass," Olive said.

Emmett looked back at her as she smiled innocently, and he started laughing.

"You're a handful," Emmett said, "that's for sure."

Olive continued to smile.

Troy sulked back to the truck and climbed into the passenger's seat. Seth was in the driver's seat now. Emmett stuck his hand out the window and rotated it in a small circle, then pulled out of the gas station and they headed back up the street. On the next block, he saw a small grocery store with only four infected out front. They did need food and this was a small town, so it would be their best option. He pulled the truck into the parking lot.

"We're gonna go check this out," Emmett said.

"I'm coming," Alexis said.

"I wouldn't expect anything less," Emmett said.

"You two okay in here alone?" Alexis asked the kids.

"It's bulletproof, right?" Felix asked.

"Yeah," Emmett said, handing Alexis the suppressed ACR.

"Then we're good," Felix said.

"We'll be right back," Alexis said.

"Don't take too long," Olive said.

They climbed out of the truck and met Greg, Lucas, and Troy, who'd already taken care of the four infected.

"Figured you'd want to hit this," Greg said.

"Looks like a good spot," Lucas said.

"There's a small hardware store out back," Troy said. "We could hit that first and get some better weapons."

"Good idea," Emmett said.

As he walked past the side of the store, an infected came around the back. It cocked its head, looking at them right before Emmett's machete entered its skull. Continuing, they arrived at the front of the tiny hardware store.

"Okay," Emmett said. "Same as last time. Greg, Alexis, backup. Lucas, Troy, let's keep it quiet."

They all nodded. Emmett banged on the door, waited, then tried to open it, but it was locked. Peering through the glass of the door, he didn't see any infected inside. Greg stepped up, brandishing the hammer, and Emmett stepped aside as Greg went to town on the door. After a few swings, he was able to batter a hole big enough to stick his hand through and unlock the door. Greg opened it and nothing came out. Emmett entered, machete held ready. It wasn't hard to check the whole store since it was just one small room. The place was clear of infected and was exactly what would be expected of a small-town hardware store. A few minutes later, they left, hauling everything they could carry. They hadn't only taken what they could use as weapons but also what might be useful further down the road.

Walking back to the vehicles, they dispersed the weapons among the adults. They'd found enough to arm everybody. The rest were put in the back of the trucks. Troy and Lucas armed themselves with axes, and they moved to the front of the grocery store. Emmett banged on the front doors and then waited. After a minute, Greg opened the door. Emmett, Lucas, and Troy were in a line in front of the door, with Alexis off to the side, able to take a shot if need be.

Infected began to pour from the store. Six of them pushed through the doors immediately. They took down three quickly, but the other three instantly took their places. Alexis fired as Greg tried to shut the door, but there were too many infected pushing against it and it wouldn't close. Greg took a few steps back and began to fire as well. Emmett had already dropped his machete and drawn his Beretta. He took down two. Lucas and Troy kept killing the infected when they made it past the doorway. As soon as it had started, it ended, with the last one coming through the door taking an axe-head to the face from Lucas. Over a dozen infected lay on the ground around the doorway.

"That worked well," Troy said, smiling.

"That it did," Emmett said.

These people were really starting to improve, not at all like when they'd first found them cowering in the elementary school. He replaced his partial magazine with a full one and picked up his machete.

Emmett entered the grocery store. The lighting was dim so he clicked on his flashlight, and the others did as well. They stayed in a group as they slowly moved through the store to the back. Once there, Emmett picked up an empty bottle of wine and threw it on the floor a little ways away. It shattered and they waited, but nothing came out.

"Buddy up and spread out. Grab anything edible that won't spoil," Emmett said.

Greg and Lucas moved off, grabbing a discarded shopping cart on their way. Emmett walked back to the front and grabbed a cart. Alexis followed, her head on a swivel. Troy trailed after her like a lost dog. The grocery store had definitely been raided, but a lot of items had fallen on the floor and no one had picked them up.

"You want to actually help?" Emmett said to Troy, throwing a dozen cans of baked beans into the cart.

Troy looked at Emmett. He'd been following behind Alexis while Emmett pushed the cart ahead and gathered all the items.

"Oh, yeah," Troy said, grabbing a bag of chips off the floor. "So Alexis, what did you do for fun before this?"

"I mainly just studied," Alexis said.

"What'd you study for?"

"My paramedic licensing exam. I'd just passed before all this went down."

"That's awesome—one of the professions that'll actually be helpful with things as they are now."

"What'd you do?"

"I worked in a bank."

"Really? I wouldn't have guessed that."

"I'm really good with numbers."

"Then how about you figure this one?" Emmett said. "What does a guy who won't shut up plus a guy with a gun equal?"

"Uhhhh," Troy said.

"Either a dead guy or a quiet guy," Emmett said, looking Troy right in the eyes.

"Yes, sir," Troy said, going back to picking up items.

"Dad," Alexis scolded quietly when Troy moved off.

"This is no time for conversation," Emmett said.

"You won't let him ride with us either," Alexis said. "Don't you like him?"

"Don't worry about that. Just watch our backs."

"Fine."

Emmett eyed Troy as he fervently picked up items now with twice the speed as before. It's not that he didn't like the kid. He just saw what he was doing here and he didn't like it. The boy needed to slow down and back off a little, maybe focus on more productive things like staying alive.

They collected three carts full of non-perishable groceries, which they loaded into boxes and then stacked those in the back of the trucks. Spending a few minutes, they handed out food to everyone. With the supplies they'd collected, it was almost like before they were captured. Almost. He was still missing all his other guns and gear, especially his M4. This ACR was nice, but it wasn't the same.

"Everyone is ready," Seth said, coming from the other truck.

"Good, time to head out," Emmett said, glancing at the group of a dozen infected heading their way from the south end of town.

Loading up, he drove out of the parking lot and the rest of the caravan followed. He grabbed a protein bar from the dash and handed one to his daughter. By the time he finished his first bar, Alexis had devoured two protein bars, a bag of chips, and a can of tuna.

"What?" she asked, noticing his look.

"I've never seen you eat that fast," Emmett said.

"I've never gone that long without eating," Alexis said.

"Good point," Emmett said, taking a bag of chips.

He glanced in the back. The kids were asleep again. Watching them, he couldn't help but yawn. How long had he been awake? Twenty-four hours? Forty-eight? Or had it been longer? He honestly couldn't remember the last time he'd gotten a good night's sleep in a real bed. It hadn't been in Safe Haven, had it? When he thought about it, he realized it very well might've been. That meant it had been over two days since he last slept. No wonder he was so tired. Maybe he'd have to try what the kids always drank. What was it called—a Monster? That seemed fitting, given everything that was going on.

Alexis was leaning against the window, looking out, and Emmett watched as the small town passed from view, replaced by gumbo hills. The different layers of clay gave the hills the look of a multilayered cake cut in half. Green ponderosa pine trees adorned some of the hills—thick in spots, sparse in others. He'd always liked this part of the country. Honestly, it was a lot like Texas in some places. Soon, Alexis joined the kids in slumber. Emmett's eyelids started to grow heavy, but he willed them to stay open. He'd had to endure a lot worse than this in the corps, so he could handle a few days without sleep now. Eyes straight ahead scanning the horizon, he settled in and the miles began to pass by.

24

A WARRIOR'S FUNERAL

"J ames!" Connor yelled, dropping to a knee and aiming toward where his brother had gone down.

Where had that shot come from?

Connor glanced at the tree line. The shot had come from closer than that. He noticed Tank turning to look behind one of the vehicles, and Connor followed his gaze. There! The first woman Connor had shot through the legs was aiming a handgun at Tank. Crosshairs settling on her, he squeezed the trigger and a bullet tore through her chest. Tank fired right after, hitting her again. Connor fired a second shot, hitting her a third time as she fell, and he fired twice more once her body rested on the ground. His knuckles were white on the foregrip of his ACR and he looked around, making sure there was no one else. None of the bodies moved. Standing up, he ran to where his brother had fallen. Tank was already there, kneeling by James.

Connor arrived and looked down at him, tears threatening to break loose. James's eyes were open, so at least he was still conscious. Connor looked down at his chest, expecting to see his shirt stained red. It wasn't. In fact, he couldn't even see James's chest because it was covered with the body armor they all wore.

"Damn," James said, sitting up. "That hurt a lot worse than I thought it would."

"You careless—" Connor said, punching James hard on the shoulder. "I thought you were dead!"

"I did, too, for a second," James said. "I forgot this heavy thing I'm wearing stops bullets."

Tank laughed. "Well, I'm glad we found 'em because it just saved your life."

"Me too," James said, standing up and wincing. "I'll have a nice bruise, and I think I reopened my side."

"A little higher and that shot would have killed you," Connor said.

"I know," James said. "Why am I always the one getting shot?"

"You must be a bullet magnet," Tank said.

James looked over to the last vehicle in line, standing stock still. "No, that can't be..."

"Your truck?" Tank asked. "Yeah, I tried to tell you that when you were going all gung-ho with the SAW."

"But... I..."

"I thought you saw it," Connor said.

James took a few steps towards his bullet-ridden white Dodge Ram.

"Oh, he SAW it, alright!" Tank said, chuckling.

Connor burst out laughing, but James barely heard them. All he could see was his majestic truck, which was now nothing more than a bullet-holder. He walked over to it, taking in the horror of the shattered windows, crooked brush guard, holes in every surface, blood on the driver's and passenger's seats, and crushed tailgate. He hadn't seen it when he was firing wildly. It was the farthest back and partially hidden from view. He did a circle around it, taking it all in. Not all of these bullets were from him. In fact, most of them weren't. His truck had been shot back at the original ambush a few days ago when Emmett was driving it, but these ones on the east-facing side weren't from him either.

"Dude," Tank said, walking up. "It's just a truck."

"No," James said. "It was more than that. We covered so many miles together. I have so many memories from that seat."

"We definitely need to get you a girlfriend," Tank said, "because that shit is creepy."

A realization dawned on him. He scrambled into the passenger's side, careful not to sit in the blood. Opening the center console, he searched inside. Buried beneath all the other stuff he kept in there, sitting like a gem in a treasure chest, was his iPod. It was undamaged. At least he had this. Grabbing a grocery bag from the holder in his door, he took all the items from inside the center console and glove box, putting them into the bag. He then went to the backseat and lifted it. Shards of glass were scattered everywhere. They'd taken the ammunition and food but left the emergency car kit, tarp, tow rope, and other such items. He grabbed those, too, taking it all over to the LAPV.

Going back, he tried to open the tailgate, but it was smashed shut and he wound up crawling in through the shattered topper window. By some miracle, their duffels of clothing, Kryptek backpacks, and other camping gear were still in there. The Reclaimers must've just been looking for the guns, ammunition, and food. Tank helped him unload all the stuff and put it into the LAPV while Chloe organized it. Connor set up on the hood of his truck, watching the tree line where the man had disappeared. It was a solemn moment for James, cleaning out the first truck he'd ever bought. He'd had it for over half a decade. He stood back, gazing at it, with Connor and Tank at either side. Movement drew James's eyes to something slithering on the floor. Was that a snake?

"Squeezer!" James exclaimed. He ran back to the truck and reached down for the snake, but it coiled around itself and hissed. He jerked his hand back. Squeezer was pissed.

"I got it, bro," Connor said, walking up behind him. "Keep an eye on the trees just in case."

"Squeezer?" Tank asked. "I thought Connor left him back in Colorado."

"He did," James said, watching his brother out of the corner of his eye as his gaze scanned the line of trees over the hood of his truck. James didn't think they had anything to worry about. That man was long gone, but he kept watch anyway. "This is another ball python we found."

"Odd coincidence," Tank said.

"That's exactly what we thought," James said.

Connor ignored the conversation and crouched down by the open back door, looking at Squeezer. Resting his hand next to the snake, he slowly slid it closer. Squeezer flicked his tongue at Connor's hand but didn't act aggressively. After a minute, Connor had a calm Squeezer in his hands.

"It just takes the right touch," Connor said.

"You've always had a way with animals," Tank said.

"Where are we going to keep him now that we don't have a cage?" James asked.

"I'll just empty one of the backpacks and put him in it," Connor said. "He'll be fine in there. I'll leave it unzipped a little for air."

He walked over to the LAPV, rummaging around in the backseat. Chloe came over from organizing the last of the stuff in the back, and Connor joined them shortly after, watching the trees.

"I think he's gone, bro," James said.

"Probably," Connor said, his eyes still scanning.

"It looks like it was a nice truck," Chloe said.

"It was," James said. "She was one of the best."

"There you go, making it all weird again," Chloe said.

"We should do something," Connor said.

"Like a funeral," Chloe said, sarcastically.

"Yes!" Tank said. "Like a warrior's funeral."

"A pyre?" James asked.

Tank pulled a grenade from his vest. "Even better."

"Oh yeah," James said. "But let me grab something quick."

Running over, he pulled out his multi-tool and unscrewed the license plates. He gazed down at the black Montana plates with a white bighorn sheep skull set in the background. The feeling of loss grew in him.

"We're good now," James said, coming back.

"If you're really doing this, we need to move the car so we don't blow it up, too," Chloe said.

"It's not a 'car,'" Tank said. "It's an armored truck... thing."

"Whatever," Chloe said, rolling her eyes.

"And we need a plan," Connor said, "so we know where we're going because this is going to draw some attention."

"All good ideas," Tank said, "but let's hurry. I'm itchin' to blow this baby up!"

"We can all agree these were the Reclaimers, right?" James asked.

"Yep," Connor said.

"And we can agree that these were their vehicles," James said, "and that they stopped here for some reason and got shot up?"

"More than likely," Tank said.

"Then where are the bodies from before?" Chloe asked.

They all looked at each other, shrugging.

"Maybe where the three came out of the trees?" Connor asked.

They walked over to the east side of the interstate and looked into the ditch. There were five bodies lying out with various gunshot wounds and holes in their heads.

"I guess that explains that," Connor said.

"So they stopped here," Tank said, "and were ambushed but then stayed here. Why?"

"Maybe it happened right before we got here and they were still licking their wounds," Connor said.

"Could be," James said. "That means that the rest of our group continued on north. Maybe Emmett stopped here to hold them off while the rest gained ground. Then he met up with them later."

"Probably," Connor said.

"Even if we're wrong on all of it," James said, "one thing is for sure. Our group isn't here and we didn't pass anybody headin' south. So they have to be headin' north."

"I think we can count on that," Tank said. "The way you guys make it sound, they'll know to wait at the border, at least for a few days."

"They should," James said.

"So that's it," Tank said. "We head north."

"That's the plan," James said. "Always was the plan. Things just keep slowing us down."

"Now that we have all that figured out," Tank said. "Let's move the rig so I can blow your truck up!"

"Can I drive it?" James asked.

"For now," Tank said. "A rebound always helps with the grieving process."

"Yes!" James said, running over and climbing into the driver's seat of the LAPV. He stuck his head back out the open door. "Bro, this thing is awesome!"

"I know," Tank said.

James drove it around the other vehicles and parked it two hundred yards north of them. He walked back and saw that Connor and Chloe had gotten down on the far side of the interstate. Tank was in the median, ready to toss the grenade and then run back.

"Ready?" Tank asked.

"Shouldn't you say something?" Chloe asked.

"Yes, I should." James was silent for a few moments, and then he smiled. "She used to be a survivor like us, until she took a bullet to the axle."

Connor and Tank chuckled.

"You're an idiot," Tank said. "But well put."

He pulled the pin on the grenade and tossed it, running back to them. It landed and rolled under the truck, coming to rest right in front of the rear axle. Tank jumped down behind the edge of the interstate, joining them. They waited for a few seconds.

The grenade exploded and shortly after, the truck. Flames sprouted towards the sky, and the sound of the blast echoed around the hills. The flames continued to spread until they had consumed the entire truck. James looked on with awe, a small piece of him truly sad that he'd lost his truck, which was ridiculous. It was just a machine, after all. But he would still miss it.

"A fitting end to a worthy steed," James said.

"Can we go now?" Chloe asked.

"Yes," Connor said, glancing at the trees.

"Time to hit the road," James said, starting to walk to the rig with the rest following. "We need to name the LAPV."

"I know," Tank said. "Scourge!"

James chuckled. "That's perfect."

"Let me guess," Chloe said. "Video game reference?"

"Pretty much," Tank said. "We are weird mofos, after all."

They loaded up into Scourge and started down I-90 again, heading north. James took off his helmet, setting it next to him as he looked out the window at the rolling hills. This may very well be the last time he ever saw Montana. While he'd been born and raised in Alaska, and later moved to Colorado, this place would always hold a special place in his heart. He'd miss the rolling plains, Ponderosa pine forests, gumbo hills, and the sunrises and sunsets that could only be seen in big sky country. Then again, he'd always liked Alaska more and was looking forward to living in the mountains again. He'd be able to hunt moose, bear, and Dall sheep. They'd finally be safe. Even with it being only eight days into the apocalypse that still seemed like a foreign concept. What would it be like to not always be on edge? As he looked out the window, his eyelids began to droop, and before he knew it, he was sound asleep.

25

SWEET GRASS

Alexis watched from the passenger's seat as her dad finished fueling up the truck. Raindrops fell against the windshield. It wasn't a downpour like the other night but more than just a light rain.

She looked around at the small town of Raynesford. There were only a couple of buildings right here by the two-pump gas station. The rest of the town—the other dozen buildings—was farther down the road. They'd been making good progress so far by staying off the interstate. There were fewer vehicles to go around and the roads were mostly clear. They'd only had to get on I-94 from Colstrip to Cowtown where they turned onto US-12. This was the first time they'd stopped since Lame Deer. Emmett and Greg had cleared the small gas station, and now the kids and adults were all in there using the restroom and stretching their legs. Away from the immediate threat of being eaten, the kids had begun to liven up. They were more like kids—playing games, annoying adults, and asking if they were there yet. They didn't even know where "there" was, but they wanted to be there, and soon.

Her dad jumped into the driver's seat, shivering as he did.

"It's raining just enough to get soaked," Emmett said.

"So what's up with you and Troy?" Alexis asked.

It was the first time they'd been alone. Olive and Felix were inside with the rest. He didn't respond right away. Instead, he pulled his truck forward, letting the next vehicle in line fill up.

"He rubs me wrong," Emmett said.

"Come on. I know it's more than that."

"Nope, that's it."

She wanted to push her dad for more information because she knew he was lying. She didn't, however. Over the years she'd learned that the more she pushed, the more he resisted. The trick was to wait until he was distracted and then ask him. That way, he'd usually respond without thinking and she'd get the truth.

The rain continued to come down outside as they fueled up all the vehicles. What would happen when gas stations ran out of fuel? There was only a limited amount. Would it take weeks? Or was there enough spread out over the country to last years? Would civilization ever stabilize enough to go back to how it was before? Or had humanity been forever changed by this event? She wondered if this was the end times she'd learned about in Sunday school, or something entirely different—just a small blip in the history of humanity.

Everyone finished fueling and using the restroom. Beverly brought Olive and Felix over to them and Alexis thanked her.

"We're all responsible for these little ones now," Beverly said. "They're our future, more so now than before."

She walked over and climbed into the passenger seat of the minivan. Everyone had switched drivers to give the others a break, but her dad climbed back into the driver's seat.

"You know I could drive for a bit and you could get some sleep," Alexis said.

"Thanks, honey, but I'm good," Emmett responded, shutting the door and starting the truck.

"I was only asking to be nice, dad," Alexis said, opening her door. "I'm either going to drive or you'll have to leave me here."

She climbed out of the truck and walked around to the driver's side. Her dad watched her standing in the rain for only a couple of seconds before he got out, grumbling. She smiled as she climbed in.

Immediately, she adjusted the seat and mirrors. Looking over at her dad, she put the truck into drive.

"I was fine," Emmett said, putting a hand over his mouth as he yawned.

"Sure," Alexis said, turning onto the highway.

"Yay!" Olive said. "Alexis gets to drive."

"Oh, great," Felix said.

"What's that supposed to mean?" Alexis asked, glancing back at him.

"You know," Felix said, looking to Emmett, "girl drivers... or... aren't they supposed to be bad or something? I hear jokes in school."

Alexis and Emmett started laughing.

"Those are just jokes," Emmett said. "Although, that is true sometimes."

"Oh," Felix said. "So we're safe with her driving?"

"Roger," Emmett said. "My daughter is a great driver. Who do you think taught her?"

"Good," Olive said. "Now, we have a game to finish."

Olive and Felix turned to each other and started playing another game of rock-paper-scissors. They were having a tournament, and Olive was up three hundred and five to two hundred and eighty. Alexis smiled at them and resumed her vigil.

"And you're positive you know the way?" Emmett asked her.

Alexis rolled her eyes. "Stay on here until we get to MT-331, take that north all the way to US-2 to avoid Great Falls. Turn west and follow that until we hit I-15 and take that all the way to the border. Yes, dad, I got it."

Emmett looked over at her, his expression pensive. "You've become a very strong and beautiful woman. I'm proud of you, Alexis. I love you."

"I love you too, daddy."

Her father beamed at her, then rested his head back and closed his eyes. That was the first time he'd ever smiled when she said "daddy." She'd always known he secretly loved it, but it also annoyed him most times. The realization made her nervous. What brought on this sudden expression of emotion from him? She hadn't seen him this open since Mason's death. Usually, in order for that to happen, something had to be going wrong. But in a way, she guessed something was wrong every day now. It was probably just because of what'd happened. He'd had to wait on the ridge all day while she could've been killed at any second. It must've taken a lot of determination not to rescue her right away. He'd waited. Then, he and Ana had rescued them all.

Ana. That woman confused the crap out of her. She still wondered if Ana had done it to save them or herself. She'd said something about a debt, and Alexis wondered if she'd been referring to them helping her in the mall. Alexis just couldn't get a read on her. She thought they'd connected so well, but it turned out they hardly had anything in common.

Ana is too selfish to have anything in common with me, Alexis thought, but felt bad as soon as she thought it.

It was just that the pain of betrayal was still too raw. Evan's death replayed in her head and she shuddered. But he'd been about to kill her. She should be thanking Ana, not hating her.

It was all because of that vile woman—Jezz. That's the one person Alexis could see herself killing. Actually, she relished the thought of Jezz on the ground, begging for her life, Alexis above her with a handgun pointed at her head...

Why was she fantasizing about that? She didn't want to end people's lives if she didn't have to. She wanted to help them. That woman just made her see red. She was pure evil. Although, what if that wasn't the whole truth? There *was* little doubt about one thing—something was definitely wrong with her. No sane person would indiscriminately kill like that. What did that say about Ana, then? Or her dad? Or James and Connor, for that matter? When they'd rescued them back in Safe Haven, they'd come in shooting anyone who was armed. And for what? To save a woman they didn't even know. Or was it because they were hurting and wanted other people to hurt?

The questions spun circles in her head as she drove past field after field. Is that all this part of the country was—fields and barren hills? Where was the "out west" she was always hearing about, the rugged mountains and all that. She'd seen some on their drive so far, but not like she'd imagined. If she remembered right, the mountains were more west from where they were. But she figured she'd be seeing plenty of mountains soon enough, living in Alaska. What would that be like—living in a remote place with only a small group of people? The peace she felt about it was unexpected. But she liked these people, and if she was going to spend the rest of her life with them, this was a pretty good group. They were just missing one—James. Connor too, she quickly added so her mind wouldn't get any ideas.

After they were established, would they try gathering more people to rebuild society? She liked that idea. They could be the foundation on which a new civilization was built. Each person would have a place, a role to play. How much of society would they replicate? Would there ever be traditional marriages again? Hopefully. That had always been one of her biggest dreams, being able to wear a white dress and walk down the aisle with her dad. She let her mind entertain the fantasy as the miles passed by.

Emmett drove down I-15 north of Shelby. They had less than an hour to the Canadian border. He'd switched with Alexis at the interstate, just in case, and she hadn't been angry at him taking control in the more dangerous situation. Once, she would have been pissed at him for taking any control from her, but she'd grown a lot in the last few years.

The sun was nearing the horizon, the rain having stopped an hour before. They were going to make it before dark as long as they didn't run into trouble. He'd told the other drivers to be ready for anything. They were going to follow his lead. If he turned around and started speeding away, so were they. If he started shooting, they would too. If he came out with his hands up, they would follow suit. He'd said that last one with no intention of doing it again. Next time, he'd go down in a blaze of glory. He glanced over at his daughter. Okay, if she was in danger, he'd surrender, but only if there was no other option.

"Do you think James and Connor made it?" Alexis asked.

Emmett looked at her. "I'd bet so."

"Where do you think they are?" Alexis asked.

"Probably either heading to, or at, the border, like we're about to be."

"I know they survived the ambush because Jezz said, 'they were invited to the party.'"

"Then they should have no problem staying alive, as long as they don't run into the other Reclaimers."

"James can handle anything," Olive said. "I'm not worried about him."

"You're right," Alexis said. "They may even be there waiting for us."

"We'll know in a few minutes," Emmett said.

"We've made good time today," Alexis said.

"It's amazing how easy it is when we're not constantly being attacked," Emmett said.

"Yeah," Alexis said, "and a lot more pleasant."

The sun sank below the horizon and the light began to fade. They should be able to see the Canadian border soon. Emmett had only been through there once before. He remembered there was a Hutterite colony west of Sweet Grass. That might be the best place to stay, depending on how bad the border was. Maybe it would just be easier to go across and wait for them in Canada.

Buildings started coming into view. They'd arrived. He continued toward the overpass. Vehicles were crashed in a haphazard line, leaving only a vehicle-size opening to go through, so he drove through the hole and under the overpass. Ahead, vehicles lined both sides of the road, effectively boxing them in. It looked like someone had cleared a path through there. Or set up a trap.

Emmett slammed on the brakes and the other vehicles slowed behind him. Was it just his imagination? After all they'd been through, he wasn't about to take any chances. He motioned out the window for the vehicles behind him to back out. Troy just looked at him, lifting his hands into the air.

Right. They don't know the damn hand signals.

Rolling down his window, he looked back to yell at Troy when movement caught his eye. There were a dozen heavily armed men in black uniforms on the overpass, standing with guns aimed down at them. They were standing next to two black, armored vehicles. Four of them held LAWs, rocket-propelled grenade launchers.

"Come out with your hands in the air!" yelled one of the men above them.

"Not again," Emmett said, slamming his hands against the steering wheel.

26

The Fight Inside

"Wake up, bro," Connor said.

James blinked, leaning away from the window. There was a rotten taste in his mouth and his shoulder was wet. He must've really been out cold to drool onto his shoulder. Taking a bottle of water, he swished it around in his mouth to wash the taste away.

"How long have I been out?" James asked.

"An hour and a half," Connor said. "We're almost to Hardin."

"Sweet," James said. "I assume nothing happened while I was out."

"Just Chloe snoring," Tank chuckled.

"I was not!" Chloe said.

"Oh, you were," Tank said.

Chloe just shook her head. Unlike before when she would have had a scowl on her face, she now wore a slight smile. Things were changing, that much was for sure.

James glanced out the windshield. It was darker now, the clouds having thickened. Small raindrops splattered on the glass, running in small lines up the windshield past the two places where bullets had hit. The impact zones were perfect circles, with streaks shooting out from them for a few inches. They almost looked like craters where a meteor had hit, just on a lot smaller scale. It was impossible to see through where they'd impacted since the glass was now white. It was a good thing Scourge was bulletproof or their plan would've needed tweaking.

"You guys think we should've done that a little differently back there?" James asked.

"We've been talking about that while you were asleep," Connor said.

"It was awesome, that's for sure," Tank said.

"I agree," James said. "But was that our best option? Even a bulletproof vehicle like this isn't invincible."

"We didn't have much of a choice," Connor said.

"What if they'd shot the windshield until it broke?" James asked.

"They would've had a hard time hitting it in the same exact place over and over again," Connor said.

"They could've gotten lucky and just blown your head off," Tank said, looking at James.

"Or thrown a grenade, like you guys did to James's truck," Chloe said.

"With how fast it happened," Tank said, "we didn't give 'em much time to react, though."

"I took out the girl with the RPG right away," Connor said. "After that, they would've had a hard time taking this thing down."

"Wait, what RPG?" James asked.

"The one that blew up the truck," Connor said. "Don't tell me you didn't notice the exploding vehicle."

"I thought..." James said.

Tank started laughing. "James thought he did that."

"What?" Connor asked, starting to laugh.

"Hey, I didn't know," James said. "I just thought..."

They all started laughing.

"The look on your face was priceless," Chloe said.

"That solves that mystery," Tank said.

"I'm glad you saw her," James said. "Otherwise, that wouldn't have ended so well."

"No, it wouldn't," Tank said.

"I had your backs," Connor said.

"We got pretty lucky," Tank said.

"It was more than just luck," James said. "We had someone watching out for us."

"In this case," Tank said, "I think you're right."

"Yeah," Connor said, glancing out the window.

"Time to suit up," Tank said. "We're here."

"Take the exit for MT-47 north," James said. "There'll be a gas station there."

"Got it," Tank said, pulling off on the exit.

"Oh, wow," James said. "That Love's is new."

"Wanna stop there and check it out?" Tank asked.

"Why?" Connor said. "We have all the food and water we can fit. All we need is fuel."

"Just wanted to make sure," Tank said.

"Let's hit the one across the street," James said.

"Guys," Chloe said. "I do need to use the restroom."

"Shat or piss," Tank asked.

"I have to piss," Chloe said.

"See," Tank said. "Even she says piss, Jamesy Boy."

"You'll have to learn to go outside," James said. "Might as well start now. We're not going in just to use the restroom. It's too risky..."

James only half heard Tank say something about showing her how. Flashes of images were burning through his mind—a blonde woman smiling at him from the back seat and the fear in her eyes, now replaced with hope; the same woman, her face pained, a gaping wound in her neck; a blood-stained face, striking blues eyes pleading to end it; a gunshot.

James was still aware of what was going on around him, but he could feel himself slipping. Images of a burning bus and a room covered in blood boiled below the surface. He tried to push back against the coming darkness as Tank pulled up to the gas station, but it was no use.

Lord, help me, James said.

Light clashed with the darkness in his mind—images of his father's body lying in a pool of blood-soaked hay and his mother barely recognizable beneath the bruising and wounds. The darkness pushed back against the light, fervent to consume him.

Jesus, heal me, James prayed desperately.

Light burst to life in his mind, burning away the darkness, sending it retreating from his mind. He sat there in the backseat, sweat covering his brow. It was gone. The darkness that had begun to grow with his parents' deaths was no more, and the healing that had started with his unusual dream a few nights ago was complete. He could feel himself, all of himself. He felt whole—better than he had in a long time—and knew in his heart that the episodes were gone. Hope had replaced the fear. James smiled.

"Yep, he's officially lost it," Tank said.

James's attention snapped back to reality, and he glanced up to see Tank and Connor staring at him.

"Another episode?" Connor asked with worry in his eyes.

"Almost," James said, joyfully. "But it'll be the last one."

"How do you know that?" Tank asked.

"Because God gave me the strength to fight the darkness," James said, remembering something he'd seen recently. "'For when I am weak, then I am strong.'"

"Good on ya, bro," Tank said. "Glad all that's over. I didn't want to have to start worryin' about you like your brother was."

Connor continued to stare at him, a calculating look on his face. His brother didn't believe he'd been healed, and James didn't blame him. All this was even a little hard for *him* to believe. The last time he'd seen that scripture was on Olive's coin purse. He prayed she was alive. The intense desire to protect her was still there inside him, even when she wasn't around. And what about Mila? Was she alive? Or Alexis? An image of those hazel eyes set in her gorgeous face and framed by brunette hair appeared in his mind. He hoped Alexis was safe.

"Ready?" Tank asked, pointing outside.

James looked out for the first time, realizing they were parked at the pumps with six zombies stumbling towards them.

"Let's do it," James said, drawing his tomahawk.

"Damn," Tank said. "I never did get one of those."

"Wait a second," James said.

He turned around and grabbed his backpack from the back seat. Opening it, he was surprised to find all his gear was still inside. Sitting on top was one of the unopened tomahawks they'd gotten from the sporting goods store in Miles. He pulled it out and showed it to Tank.

"Oh hell, yeah," Tank said. "I might just kiss ya for that."

James handed him the tomahawk. "Please don't."

"Fine, but only because you asked nicely," Tank said, ripping open the packaging. "This'll do."

He pulled the tomahawk out of its sheath and stepped out of Scourge. James and Connor jumped out after him. The canopy over the gas pumps kept most of the rain off. Tank already had two zombies down before James slammed a tomahawk into his first zombie's eyes and it fell to the ground. Connor dropped one next to him, and then there were just two more in front of them. The brothers stood side-by-side, tomahawks raised, ready to take down the last two only a few yards away.

With a cry of, "Leeeeeroy Jenkins!" Tank ran at the two zombies from the side. The first one took a tomahawk to the face and Tank spun around, jerking the point out and using the momentum to slam it into the other one. Its skull caved from the force of the blow. Tank stood there, panting, with blood speckling his face.

"Damn, that's fun," Tank said, glancing over at the brothers. "What? You guys always get to have all the fun. I didn't even get to shoot a single Reclaimer. It was my turn."

"That was very impressive," James said. "especially with that little pirouette in there."

"You're just jealous because of how badass I am," Tank said, walking back to the rig.

"A little," James admitted.

"I don't understand why you guys don't have girls hanging off each arm," Chloe said, getting out. "I mean with your maturity, sophisticated conversations, and non-video-game quotes, I just don't get it."

"If girls only knew what was hidden below all this joking around—" Tank began to say but was cut off by Chloe.

"They'd run in fear," she said.

"Exactly," Connor said.

Chloe began to laugh but her smile faltered when she registered the serious look on his face. Then Connor broke out with a smile and the three of them started laughing.

"Sometimes I wonder if cutting my own leg off and going out on my own would be better," Chloe muttered.

"You could try it," Tank said. "I'll keep your leg."

"What?" James asked, laughing. "You'll keep her severed leg?"

"Sure," Tank said. "I'd find a use for it."

They all started laughing at the absurdity of the comment.

"You're a real piece of work," James said.

"I think we all are," Connor said.

"True," James said.

"So," Chloe said, after the laughter had settled down and Tank had begun to fuel up, "about that bathroom..."

"There's some TP in the stuff we stole from the hilltop," James said.

"We didn't *steal* anything," Connor corrected. "We just tactically acquired it."

"Plus, they were all dead," Tank said. "Most of them, anyway."

"I already have some," Chloe said. "I mean where do I go? You guys are standing right here."

"We'll all go to the other side of Scourge," James said, "and you do what you need to do."

"Okay," Chloe said, hesitantly. "Get over there then!"

James moved to the other side to join Tank, and Connor stepped next to him. They stood facing away from the vehicle.

"If I catch any of you looking, I'll castrate you," Chloe said.

"Damn," Tank muttered.

After a few seconds of silence, Chloe said, "Can you turn some music on or something?"

"But I can't turn around," Tank said. "I like my genitals."

"Go ahead and turn around. I'm just standing here," Chloe said.

"Just keep an eye out," Connor said. "The noise may attract some zombies. We'll watch our side."

"I will," Chloe said. "Now, some music."

James glanced back to see Chloe standing on the other side, an annoyed look on her face. Tank opened the driver's door and turned the key to auxiliary. He grabbed his iPod, and after a few seconds, *This is War* by Teamheadkick started playing.

"Better?" Tank asked.

"Louder," Chloe said. "This is hard enough as it is."

Tank cranked up the volume. Chloe gave them a thumbs-up and then motioned for them to turn back around. They obliged. James started laughing as the band started singing about bashing zombies' heads in. Halfway through the song, the music turned off.

"What the hell music was that?" Chloe asked from the passenger's side.

"Why'd you turn it off?" James asked. "It was just getting to the good part."

"Please don't tell me that was a video game thing," Chloe said. James looked at Tank and Connor, and then shrugged. "You're hopeless. I didn't even know there was such a thing."

"Oh yeah. Video game raps are kick ass," Tank said as he topped off the tank.

Chloe rolled her eyes.

"Now that we're fueled up," James said, "we should probably go inside and clean our wounds."

Connor nodded, grabbing one of the first aid kits they'd taken from the hilltop.

"What!" Chloe shouted. "I just pissed on the pavement outside and you intended to go in the whole time?"

"Yeah... Well, no," James said. "We weren't always going to go in. I just thought of it."

"I really hate you guys sometimes," Chloe said, storming into the far back seat.

"I'll stay," Tank said.

James hadn't meant to do it that way, but it was becoming more apparent by the minute that he needed to clean his wounds and get fresh bandages on them. Light rain fell as they walked up to the door, speckling James's glasses. Even with his hat on, the wind was blowing just enough to get rain underneath. If only he'd switched to contacts before all this. But what if he ran out? Or lost one in the middle of combat? He'd been blessed so far that his glasses hadn't broken with everything going on. It would be a horrible day when they did, although he did have an extra pair in his backpack and another pair in the plastic bag of stuff from his truck. But that'd still suck.

Arriving at the front of the gas station, they banged on the door a few times and then opened it. Nothing came out. Connor took point and James followed. The inside was trashed, as they'd come to expect. Moving to the back of the station, they entered the men's restroom. The Band-Aids were still good on Connor's shoulder so they left them. James took off his armor and shirt, wincing.

"Does your side hurt?" Connor asked.

"No," James said. "My sunburn."

"Toughen up, you wimp," Connor said.

James ignored him. His side had sealed and ripped open a few times over the last day, and his bandage was soaked through again. Connor spent the next few minutes doctoring James's wounds, and James left the gas station feeling much better. His ear and side ached from the cleaning, but the fresh bandages felt better than the sticky old ones and they smelled ten times better. He climbed into the back seat of Scourge and sighed.

"You gentlemen need a ride?" Tank asked.

"Yes, sir," James said.

"Where to?" Tank asked.

"Somewhere far away from here," Connor said.

"On it," Tank said, taking the ramp for the interstate.

They passed a zombie in the other lane. It stumbled after them, trying to catch up.

"Damn," Tank said. "I should've run it over."

"What were you thinking?" Connor asked.

"I was busy pickin' our next song," Tank said.

"You know that's why you make a playlist," Chloe said. "So you're not on your iPod when you're driving."

"He always does it," James said. "If he can drive in FoCo with traffic, then we're plenty safe on the interstate with zombies."

"Found it," Tank said. "This is for us boys. To the good 'ole days."

These Are The Days by The Exies played and James was taken back to a different time—before the apocalypse and before the three of them had gone their separate ways in life, back to when they were still in high school. They looked at each other and smiled. They'd been through a lot over the years, and through thick or thin, they'd always stuck together. The apocalypse sure as hell wasn't going to tear them apart now.

"I love you guys," James said.

"And that just killed the moment," Tank joked. "But really, I'm glad we're together for this."

"Awww," Chloe said.

"I'll deny I ever said that, so don't even think about repeatin' it," Tank said.

"I'm glad we're all here, too," Connor said.

"This was how it was meant to be," James said. "The three of us together at the end of all things."

"Excuse me?" Chloe asked.

"Four of us," Tank corrected.

"Better," Chloe said.

James smiled, glancing at his brother and best friend, then back at Chloe. They'd been through so much in the last eight days, loss after loss, and it seemed like nothing could go right. It was like they were trapped on some carnival ride of horror, one bad thing right after another—losing their parents, finding a new group and losing most of them, then being captured by a lunatic, defeating the last of the Reclaimers, and now here they were, broken but stronger than ever, wounded but full of hope. Maybe, just maybe, they could all survive long enough to make it to Alaska and start a new life.

The interstate stretched before them and he could see for miles. On both sides, endless fields of green grass, hay, and other crops covered the landscape. The world was still full of life. The plants and animals had been affected very little. They just had a new predator to be wary of. The planet was still spinning, the sun still rising, everything still surviving as it always had been for centuries. They could move on, too. No matter what was thrown at them, they would face it. Even with all that had happened over the past few days, James had found his hope again.

27

First Occurrence

C onnor watched out the window as the last of Great Falls faded from view. If they could make this kind of progress all the way to Alaska, they might actually be able to make it in a few days, but that wouldn't happen. Something was bound to go wrong soon. That's how this worked now.

Just when you thought you were safe or making headway, Connor thought, *boom! The universe knocks you down.*

That was what was happening here. God was either punishing them for something or turning a blind eye to everything. If there even was a God. Funny, he'd never really questioned it before. As he thought about it, he realized he had briefly a few times, but mostly he went along with it, believing without proof. Then he was medically discharged from the corps, the one place he wanted to be and the job he'd wanted to do until he was either too old or dead. What more could life be about than giving all of yourself for your country to protect those you loved? He'd been ready for that. As an infantryman, he'd had to be. He'd truly been ready to take a bullet for the brother in line next to him.

Then it had all been taken away because of one injury. Now he was glad it'd happened the way it had because it allowed him to be here with James and Tank. This *was* where he was meant to be. So maybe

God did have a plan for that, but what about all the rest? Their parents were dead and they were continually met with resistance, no matter what they did or where they went. It was like they weren't supposed to go to Alaska. But what did that leave them with? Sitting down and curling up into a ball? Hell no. He'd keep fighting until there was no air left in his lungs. He was still ready to give his life in defense of his brothers. Only the battlefield had changed, not the truth in his heart. He was a warrior, and no injury would take that away.

The miles continued to pass by as Connor was absorbed in his thoughts. James had talked about God protecting them earlier. Did Connor still believe that? If he was honest with himself, he did. That didn't mean he wasn't pissed at God for all this. It did mean he knew God still had their backs. That hadn't changed; it was just hard to see sometimes. How could it not be? They were living in a world where people's corpses came back from the dead to slaughter the living. There were people running around killing others for no better reason than they wanted to. Where was God in all that?

Where He's always been, a part of Connor's mind said.

The world had changed countless times over the centuries—between wars, natural disasters, and mass genocide. Through that time God had stayed the same. He knew God couldn't intercede in every conflict or else where would free will be? Was this any different than war or anything else the world had faced since its creation? God had destroyed the face of the earth once with a flood. Maybe this was like that. But if so, that meant it was going to get a lot worse before it got better. So be it. Connor would rise to face whatever challenges came his way. His brother was alive and mostly unharmed. He had his best friend and enough supplies to last them for weeks. Throw in a large arsenal and an almost indestructible vehicle, and they had a fighting chance.

The sun had set and the sky was beginning to darken. They wouldn't make it to the border before nightfall. Fortunately, the rain had stopped.

"How were you so convincing last night?" Tank asked, glancing back at Chloe.

"I made myself think I really saw something," Chloe said, moving up to the middle seat. James scooted over to give her room. "It wasn't that hard. I was legit freaked being out there in the dark."

"You're good," James said. "I was even freakin' out."

"Thanks," Chloe said. "It didn't hurt that I was taking theater classes in college."

"Now, that makes sense," Tank said.

"Speaking of last night, we forgot to read this!" James exclaimed and held up Bryce's journal.

"What're you waitin' for?" Tank asked. "Get readin'!"

James opened the journal, turned to the end, and then flipped back a few pages.

"June 22nd. We've been called in. That isn't supposed to happen. That's why I signed up for this division, so I could spend more time with Elliot. The call went out this morning, something about an occurrence down in Texas. Other teams have already been down there for a few days, but we're supposed to go up to Sheridan. They said they might have an occurrence up there too. We leave in an hour. I better pack."

"Wait," Tank said. "Wasn't that like two days before they announced the outbreak?"

"Yeah," Chloe said. "They announced it on the twenty-fourth."

"And he said they already had teams down in Texas before that," Connor said.

"Damn," James said. "They did know."

"I told you," Tank said. "Our government has a lotta secrets."

"Keep readin'," Connor said.

James looked back down and continued reading. *"June 23rd. The First Response Team went in and found the man. Looks like it was an occurrence. That's not good. I heard them talking about there being more popping up all over. The whole country is infected. How did that happen? How am I going to protect Elliot if the world is going to hell? My worry may be for nothing. The higher-ups are saying they have it under control. I hope so. Otherwise, we're all screwed.*

"June 26th. Two days. Two days ago they announced it. The world is coming to an end. Two days and everyone is dead. I don't even know how

it happened or how they got past our defenses, but they did somehow. Got right into the bunk tent and started tearing them apart. I was able to hide Elliot. He survived. I don't know what I would've done if he hadn't survived. But he did. He did.

"June 27ᵗʰ. I don't think any got in. I couldn't find a body. If I had to guess, I'd say some of our own turned. Don't ask me how, but they did. Maybe they were infected when they went into town, or... something else. I don't understand how this works. I'm not a scientist!

"June 28ᵗʰ. One of the guys showed back up today. I swore I saw him get taken down the other night. But I can't trust my eyes. I've been seeing some weird stuff lately, not sure if it's something to be worried about. Elliot doesn't think so. Anyway, Lateno walked right in and sat down on his bunk. He asked where his stuff was, said he needed it. So I went out and got it for him. When I came back, half of my teammates were sitting on their bunks. Spent the whole day getting their gear for them. Lazy pricks didn't want to get it themselves. I am the newbie, though.

"June 29ᵗʰ. They're all dead. I don't know what I saw the other day but they're all dead. I want to leave this place, but Elliot doesn't want to. He says it's not safe and he's scared to leave. I could just tell him we need to go, but then he'd start screaming and I can't stand it when he screams. It feels like my head is going to explode. We'll stay, for Elliot."

"First off," Tank said, "that dude *was* batshit. Secondly, screw our government! If they'd just given us a heads up, maybe things would be different."

"Maybe," Connor said.

"Why would they hide it?" Chloe asked.

"Because they're involved," Tank said.

"They did know about it long before anyone else did," James said.

"Are we even sure it was our government?" Connor asked. "Could be private contractors working with a company. Those uniforms were bare of any rank and insignia, and all the nametags seemed like nicknames."

"You know what?" Tank said. "That may be exactly it. I've been assuming it was our government, but they didn't seem any more prepared than us. What if it's a private company, like the Umbrella Corporation?"

"If it's anything like that, we're screwed," James said.

"Video game," Chloe guessed.

"And movies," Tank said.

"And books," Connor said.

"I get it," Chloe said.

"Raccoon City, Hill City," Tank said. "They do sound kinda similar."

"I sure as hell hope it's not the t-virus," James said.

"That'd be just what we need," Connor said.

"We'd all be dead in less than a week," Tank said.

"I really don't even wanna know," Chloe said. "This is bad enough."

"Yes, it is," Connor said.

So someone knew about this beforehand. Of course they did. How else would it spread like this? It was either a horrible accident or a planned attack. But who would cause this kind of destruction? There'd be nothing left after the zombies killed everyone. Not a very good war tactic. It could be terrorists and they just wanted to wipe America off the face of the earth. Did it even matter in the end? It'd happened, one way or another. Now they just had to live through it. Who cared how it started. It only mattered how it would end, which would be them in Alaska—soon.

"This would make a great title for a book," Tank said, turning up the volume.

Bad Company by Five Finger Death Punch played through the sound system.

"Yeah, it would," James said. "If I ever wrote a book, I'd call it *Bad Company*. It'd be about these three badass characters that went around kickin' ass and takin' names!"

"I'd read that book," Tank said.

"I may even read it," Chloe said. "Would there be any romance?"

"Of course," James said. "Every good book needs a little romance in it."

"There'd be a ton of guns," Connor said.

"And all kinds of explosions," Tank said.

"At least one on every page," James said.

"Sounds like you guys should make this an action movie instead of a book," Chloe said.

"That'd come after the book became a bestseller," James said.

"Maybe we should all three write it," Tank said.

"I can see it now," James said. "*Bad Company* written by The Wolf Pack."

"That'd be a damn good book," Tank said.

"Too bad none of you became writers," Chloe said.

"It *is* sad," James said. "But why write it when we can just live it?"

"We did just take on thirteen guys and blow up not one, but two, trucks," Tank said.

"I know it had to look awesome when we were driving down the interstate, while I fired the SAW wildly from the top," James said.

"That could be the cover of our book!" Tank said.

"Man, that sounds awesome," Connor said, smiling.

The end of the world and here he was with his two best friends and brothers. It was almost perfect. If they could just find somewhere safe, they might have a chance at a normal life.

"What the hell!" Chloe screamed from the backseat.

Tank pressed on the breaks, Scourge coming to a screeching halt. Connor drew his handgun, looking back at Chloe, and James had drawn his knife. Her eyes were glued to the floor where Squeezer was slithering up from the rear of the vehicle.

"What's a snake doing in here?" Chloe asked, her feet pulled up to her chest.

James started laughing and soon the other two joined in.

"Dicks," Chloe said, clearly not amused.

"That's Squeezer," Connor said, reaching back and picking him up.

"What?" Chloe asked, glaring at them.

"We found him a few days ago," James said. "He was in my truck when the Reclaimers took it, and he was still there earlier."

"I had him in a backpack," Connor said. "He must've gotten out."

"You're kidding me!" Chloe said. "A pet snake at the end of the world?"

"Why not?" James asked.

"I take it you don't like snakes?" Tank asked, a mischievous glint in his eye.

"Don't you even dare!" Chloe said, staring daggers at him.

"Don't worry, I won't," Tank said.

"You better not," Chloe said, "or I'll kill you."

Connor turned forward, putting Squeezer around his neck. The snake liked the heat from his skin and was content to ride there as Tank started down the interstate again, chuckling to himself. Connor would need to find a cage or something to put him in at their next stop. If he thought Squeezer would stick around, he'd keep him loose in the rig, but being an animal he would probably just leave. Or someone would step on him. He didn't want to admit it, but he was growing fond of the snake.

"Keep that thing up there," Chloe said, putting her legs back down.

"I'll empty out one of the totes of protein bars," James said, climbing into the back.

"Good idea," Connor said.

After a few minutes, James had a passable snake cage. The tote had small holes poked into the lid and a piece of a blanket covering the bottom. Inside was a small box for Squeezer to curl up in and a plastic water bottle cut in half. He had cover and water, and they'd get some kind of heat source for him next time they stopped. Luckily, a ball python could go months without food, so they were good on that for now. Connor passed Squeezer back to James, who set him in the bottom of the makeshift cage. Squeezer slowly slithered around, flicking his tongue out to test his new environment. James set the tote in the farthest backseat and buckled it in.

"There," he said.

"Thanks, bro," Connor said.

"That better, Chloe?" Tank asked, smiling.

"Actually, yes," she said. "At least I don't have to worry about him going up my leg or anything."

"Here," James said, handing out a couple protein bars to everyone.

"Thanks," Chloe said.

They ate in silence. The border was only a few miles away and they all knew it. James checked to make sure he had a round in the chamber and a full magazine in. Then he examined his kit to confirm it was fully loaded and his handgun was secure on his hip.

"Eyes up," Tank said.

"What'd the sign say?" Connor asked.

"We're only a mile out," Tank said.

"Time to see if they made it," James said.

"If they didn't?" Chloe asked.

"Then we continue on," James said. "I just pray they did."

"Stay frosty," Connor said. "Could be anything up there."

In the End by Black Veil Brides began to play through the speakers as they continued on. Headlights cut through the darkness and illuminated the interstate ahead. They were approaching an overpass. Sitting in front of it was a small wreck, with a perfectly sized gap in it. Tank slowed the rig to squeeze through. It almost looked like there were lights up past the border, but that couldn't be right, could it?

"That was a little..." James started to say but stopped as he saw the headlights shining on a perfect path through walls of vehicles leading to the border crossing.

"Conveniently placed," Connor said.

"Trap?" Tank said, slowing.

"Probably," James said. "We should back out."

"On it," Tank said and threw the vehicle into reverse.

Scourge sped backward and Tank slammed on the brakes. At the end of the path, blocking the way back out, was a vehicle identical to theirs.

"Shit!" Tank said. "They found us!"

"Gun it!" Connor said. "Let's take our chances at the crossing."

Tank slammed it back into drive and stepped on the gas.

"Get ready," James said, picking up the SAW.

They flew through the wall of vehicles, every once in a while scraping the sides, sending sparks flying. The other vehicle didn't chase them, which was a bad sign.

"I knew something like this would happen," Connor said.

They burst from the tunnel of vehicles and looked ahead at the customs gates. Only two were open and there were spike-strips laid across both. Tank slammed on the brakes, causing the vehicle to slide to a stop. Out of the building to their left poured two dozen fully outfitted men, wearing the same uniforms the Wolf Pack wore. The men spread out, effectively surrounding them.

"I think we'll get some answers as to who these people are soon," James said.

"That or they'll kill us on sight," Connor said.

"Well, hell," Tank said. "They have rocket launchers."

"And a sniper in that glass room over by the gates," Connor said. "Probably anti-tank rounds if they're prepared."

"I'd guess they are," James said.

"Get out of the vehicle, now!" shouted one of the men.

"Damn," Chloe muttered.

"We don't have much of a choice," James said, laying down the SAW and putting his hands in the air. The rest of them followed suit.

28

IN THE END

J ames sat in a small, unadorned room in the back of the US customs building. It was just like in all the movies. He was handcuffed and sitting in a chair with a table between him and an empty chair. There was a mirror on the wall and there would be someone behind that, watching him.

He was waiting for someone to interrogate him. The good thing was that at least this room was safe. A zombie would be hard-pressed to get in there past all the guards. Plus, it did seem that the uniformed men were either part of the government or working with them, which made him oddly calm. There was no threat of zombies and he was in the custody of the US and, maybe, Canadian militaries.

James and the others hadn't taken any action against them and would hopefully be released after telling their story, especially when the government learned they didn't want to stay. But he didn't want them seizing all their gear or Scourge. How long had he been sitting in here anyway? It had to have been at least a half hour. What were they doing out there? Searching all their stuff?

The door opened and man in a gray suit walked in

"I would offer to shake your hand, but..." James said, holding up his handcuffed wrists.

"No need, Mr. Andderson," the man said, sitting down.

"I see you already talked to my friends, Mr..." James said.

"Yes, Chloe was very cooperative," he said. "You can call me Mr. Smith."

Really? James thought, *That's the best he could do?*

"I'd love to get this sorted out and be on our way," James said.

"Good. State your name."

"You already know my name."

"Humor me."

"James Andderson."

"How many are in your group?"

"You know that, too."

"Answer the questions."

"Four of us."

"What are their names?"

James clenched the arms of his chair with white knuckles. "Connor, Tank—"

Mr. Smith cut him off. "Full names."

James ground his teeth. "Connor Andderson, Allen Hook, and Chloe. I don't know her last name."

"Where were you heading?"

"Alaska. Ever heard of it?"

"What did you do before all this?" Mr. Smith asked.

"I was a hunting guide, but now we in the killin' zombie business. And cousin, business is a-boomin'!"

"Is that a line from a movie?"

"Mostly," James said, fuming, "and as long as you plan on asking these stupid questions, I'll keep quoting movies. Stop wasting both our time and just ask me what you really wanna know."

"I see you lack patience."

"No, I don't have much patience for pointless questions from some guy in a suit while my friends and I are being held against our will, for what? Surviving? I have no patience for that."

"Fine Mr. Andderson, have it your way. How did you come by all that gear and the LAPV?"

"A much better question..." James said and told him the story, starting with the Reclaimers taking their friends and ending with them arriving here.

"I see," Mr. Smith said.

"Have you had anyone else come through lately?" James asked. If they greeted everyone like this, they may have seen the rest of their group.

"I'm not at liberty to say."

"Anyone named Anastasia Romanovski? Or Alexis and Emmett Wolfe?"

"I'm not at liberty to say."

"It's the end of the damn world. Cut the shit and just tell me."

"I can't. Now if you could tell me—" Mr. Smith cut off, raising a hand to his ear. He acted like he was listening to someone talk for a few seconds. "If you'll excuse me."

Mr. Smith stood up and headed for the door.

"That's it?" James asked. "You gonna let me go?"

"Not at this time," Mr. Smith said, shutting the door behind him.

"Come on!" James said to the closed door. Then he looked at the mirror. "I know you're in there. Just get me someone who can tell me what's going on. We don't want to cause any trouble; we just want to be on our way!"

Nothing happened and no one answered. He waited for another few minutes, then decided to use the time to his advantage. If he couldn't do anything else, maybe he could catch up on some sleep. Resting his hands on the table, he laid his head on top of them. It wasn't extremely comfortable, but he was tired enough that he was soon asleep.

The bang of the door opening woke him. A man in Marine woodland cammies walked into the room, while two other Marines stood outside holding M16s.

"Stand up, please," the Marine said. James obliged and the Marine unlocked his handcuffs. "Follow me."

"Yes, sir," James said, following behind the Marine. "Where are we going?"

"Out."

The other two Marines fell into step behind James. At least he was free now. Anything was better than being trapped in that room.

They walked down the hallway in the opposite direction from where they'd first come in. At the end, they turned and climbed a set of stairs, then walked down another hallway, turned, and exited the building. He was in a parking lot with a chain link fence behind him and to his left. Streetlights illuminated the parking lot. Connor, Tank, and Chloe were inside one of the pools of light, unrestrained.

"Wait here," the Marine said, getting into a Jeep and driving off. The other Marines stood at attention by the door leading inside.

"Glad you're alive, bro," Connor said as James walked over.

"Any idea what's goin' on?" Tank asked. "They didn't even talk to me."

"Me neither," Connor said.

"He talked to me just for a bit, but then he left the room after I told him about how we got the gear," James said.

"He talked to me for a while," Chloe said. "I didn't know if I should lie or not, so I just told him the truth."

"Good call," James said. "No reason not to cooperate."

He looked around. They seemed to be on the Canadian side of Sweet Grass. A street ran to their right for a few blocks and the lights were working. In fact, the whole town was lit up. In front of them, about seven hundred yards away, looked to be a wall around the town. It seemed to be made of a solid block at the base, five or six feet high, with another four feet of metal fence with deterrent wire on top. If he had to guess, this wall surrounded the whole town, or at least the part they were in. A thumping sound drew his attention. He glanced around, looking up at the sky. It grew louder.

"That has to be a chopper," Connor said.

A few seconds later, a Black Hawk helicopter flew over, coming from the east. It went a few hundred yards in front of them and landed in what looked like a baseball field. One of the black LAPVs, like the one they had, drove up to it and some men in black uniforms loaded ten civilians with suitcases onto it. The Black Hawk immediately took off and flew south.

"Wow," Tank said. "So this is the real deal."

"I think so," James said.

"It looks like they have a fully operational base here," Connor said.

A black truck turned onto the street they were on and headed their way. The truck looked familiar. It had bars on the windows and—was that a shooting bench on the topper?

"Emmett!" James exclaimed.

"Well, I'll be damned," Connor said. "They actually made it."

"I'll finally get to meet the people I've been hearin' all about," Tank said.

Emmett pulled up right in front of them. Alexis jumped out of the passenger seat and came around to meet them. Was it just the lighting or did she look even more beautiful than James remembered? She rushed over to James and, for a second, he almost bolted. Women were scarier than zombies, after all. Instead, he took two steps forward and wrapped his arms around her. They hadn't known each other for long at all and hadn't... her hair smelled nice. The feeling of her body pressed tight against his caused him to forget all rational thought, and he didn't want this moment to end, ever.

Someone cleared their throat and James looked up to see Emmett glaring at him from behind his daughter. James reluctantly broke the embrace.

"I was worried about you," Alexis said, suddenly fidgeting with a strand of loose hair. "I'm glad you're safe." She moved to Connor and gave him a quick hug—a lot quicker than the one she'd given him.

"I'm glad you're alive, sir," James said, shaking Emmett's hand.

"Same goes for you two," Emmett said.

The glare was still in his eyes, but he had a smile on his face as well. What did that mean? Was he going to murder James in his sleep for hugging his daughter like that? It was just a hug. Suddenly, he was more afraid of what was inside the fence than outside of it.

"This is Tank and Chloe," James said.

"Nice to meet you," Alexis said, shaking each of their hands.

"You, too," Chloe said.

"Pleasure," Emmett said, doing the same.

"Pleasure's all mine," Tank said.

"Where's our gear?" Connor asked.

"And my vehicle?" Tank asked.

"They'll keep it for now, but Saul—excuse me, Captain Miller—said we can discuss what to do tomorrow after you're settled," Emmett said.

"Speaking of," James said. "Why'd they release us?"

"Captain Miller was watching your interview," Emmett said. "When you said my name, he came to me and asked about you guys. I vouched for you, so you better be on your best damn behavior."

"Yes, sir," the four of them said.

James and Connor looked at Tank.

"What?" Tank asked. "Why're you lookin' at me?"

"Best behavior," James said.

"C'mon," Tank said. "I'm always on my best behavior."

"Did you know the captain before?" Connor asked.

"We served in Iraq together," Emmett said, "although he wasn't a captain then."

"Where's Olive? And the rest of the group?" James found himself asking.

"She's safe," Alexis said, then hesitated. "But we have some catching up to do."

"How many?" James asked.

"A couple," Alexis said, "but it's not as bad as it could be."

"Come on," Emmett said. "Let's head back to the house and get you settled."

Emmett climbed into his truck and Alexis took Chloe around to the passenger side. James, Connor, and Tank stood outside for a few seconds, processing all that had just happened. They were safe in a walled town within the protection of the United States military. Apparently, they had a house and might even get their gear back. They'd been thrown a huge curveball, but for once it was a good thing.

"Let's go," James said, putting an arm around each of his brothers as they walked towards the truck.

"We finally did it, boys," Tank said.

"Yes, we did," Connor said.

"We ride together," James said.

"We die together," Connor said.

"Badass brothers for life," the three of them said in unison.

EPILOGUE

Z eke stood on the side of the road, rifle in his hands. The burning wreckage of a white truck lit the night sky in a fiery glow, which perfectly matched his attitude. He hadn't seen them blow up the vehicle, but he'd heard it. Those punks! How had three *boys* done this? They'd taken down a dozen of their group. And how? By charging in like a bunch of imbeciles. They'd left one to snipe. That had been a smart move, but that was their only smart move. Luck, that's all it had been. Well, their luck would turn soon. When she got back, she'd be furious. If he wasn't one of her top lieutenants, he'd be worried for his safety. As it was, he worried about the poor saps who were with her. She wouldn't kill Max, but the other two—Frank and Terg—she wouldn't hesitate to reclaim them in a fit of rage.

After he'd realized they were going to kill the rest of his group, he'd dashed into the trees. He could've stayed and maybe gotten one or two, but he didn't. It wasn't worth his life to try and avenge the death of people he cared nothing for. So he'd gone into the cut and waited until they left. Then he'd come back, once it was safe. When Jezz found those three again, the roles would be reversed and they'd be the ones slaughtered.

He bent down, continuing to gather all the weapons strewn about. That was another of their imbecilic moves. They'd left all the firearms. Then again, considering how well they were armed, they might not have needed them, but they still should've picked them up. He finished, setting the last of them down in the bed of the remaining truck. Jumping on the tailgate, he sat there, waiting. His mind began to drift.

He let it.

The others had been talking about a fiery redhead who'd killed two of her own. Then she'd broken out, killing one with a fork, then six more with a knife, before rescuing her group. That made sense to him—killing two to save them all. Jezz couldn't wrap her mind around it, though. She kept thinking if the redhead was willing to kill, wanted to kill, then she would stay with the Reclaimers and kill. Jezz was wrong, of course. She was a smart woman and a decent leader, but she couldn't think outside the box. Everything was black or white for her, but in reality, life was varying shades of gray.

That redhead was presumably the same one who had lured them away from their real targets and set up this ambush. It was painfully obvious to him now. It hadn't been earlier, not to any of them. If he'd known the details of her escape before or met her in person, it might've been different. Then he could've known what she would've done, but he was out at the ambush all day and never even saw the woman. Besides her red hair, some said she was Russian. He would believe that when he saw her. Whatever or whoever she was, he had to respect her. She did what needed to be done to survive and she did it well. What if she was—

He killed that thought before it could spawn in his head. There was no room for rogue thoughts.

Headlights shone ahead on the interstate, heading south towards him. That would be her. He stood up, walking to the other side of the truck. The SUV was speeding down the interstate. She was already angry. It swerved around the side of the blockade, going into the ditch and sending dirt flying behind it. It screeched to a halt next to the flaming truck. Zeke walked over to meet her.

Jezz stepped out of the black SUV and stalked over to him. Max and Frank got out and followed, stopping a couple of paces behind her. Terg was gone.

"Where is everyone?" she asked.

"Dead," Zeke said in his heavy Russian accent.

"All of them?" she hissed.

"Da," Zeke said.

Jezz turned quicker than any of them—save Zeke—could react. She drew her knife and lunged on Frank, driving it into his chest. He barely put up a fight as she continued to drive the knife into his heart—once, twice, two dozen times. She stood up, wiping the blood from the blade on her pants. When she turned to face Zeke, specks of blood showed on her face and shirt. Her smile sent shivers down his spine. Nothing else could do that.

"What happened?" she asked in a much calmer tone.

"Three men attacked us," Zeke said. "They were the brothers, I think, and the big man from three nights ago."

"Ah," Jezz said, "so they came for their group and killed all of my Reclaimers. They will have to pay for this."

"We haven't had somethin' this bad happen since those rich kids escaped," Max said.

"No, Max," Jezz said. "This is a lot worse than six brats escaping our ambush."

"Did you find her?" Zeke asked.

"No," Jezz spat. "We lost her in the mountains to the south. There were too many roads and she is clever."

"What do we do now?" Max asked.

"They must be reclaimed," Jezz said. "Everyone else can wait, but those three must be reclaimed above all."

"So we hunt?" Zeke said, lifting his rifle.

"Yes," Jezz said, absently caressing the edge of her blood-smeared knife. "We hunt."

Acknowledgements

This may be getting a little redundant but as always, I couldn't have finished this book without the help of numerous people. Huge thanks to:

Jesus, you keep lighting the path before me and helping me along the way I'm meant to tread.

My wife, your constant love and support allows me to continue to write!

My family, your continued support is amazing.

Guildies in the FRG, you guys just keep helping me make these stories better and better!

My awesome editor, to say you are a HUGE part in making these books readable is an understatement!

My cover artist, well done man, you outdid yourself this time!

And last, but certainly not least, all my readers. I know I've said this before, but without you guys and gals I'd never be able to keep doing this!

About the Author

Joshua is a Jesus Freak and adventurous nerd, who loves the outdoors. He's the award-winning and best-selling author of the zombie apocalypse series, *The Brother's Creed*. When he's not escaping into the mountains, he can be observed living in Northern Wisconsin with his wife, two sons, guns and katanas. He has a love for all things imaginary and finds inspiration in the wilderness, away from the distractions of life. He's currently pursuing a career as an indie author and writing coach. Some of his other passions include hunting, shooting, board & video games, hard rock, reading, and anything fantasy & sci-fi.

Learn more at:

joshuacchadd.com

ALSO BY JOSHUA C. CHADD

The Brother's Creed Series
Outbreak
Battleborn
Wolf Pack
Bad Company
Last Hope

To see more, scan below or visit:

joshuacchadd.com/books

More from Publisher

Be sure to check out our other great science fiction and fantasy stories at:

bladeoftruthpublishing.com/books